Feng Shui Mysteries by Denise Osborne

A DEADLY ARRANGEMENT
POSITIONED TO DIE
DESIGNED TO KILL

DESIGNED
TO KILL

Denise Osborne

BERKLEY PRIME CRIME, NEW YORK

DESIGNED TO KILL

A Berkley Prime Crime Book / published by arrangement with the author

PRINTING HISTORY
Berkley Prime Crime mass-market edition / March 2003

ISBN: 0-425-18911-2

PRINTED IN THE UNITED STATES OF AMERICA

10 9 8 7 6 5 4 3 2 1

This book is dedicated to the Good Ch'i Elves
for their generous contributions to the
author and the work:
Christopher James Osborne, Alberta Barker,
Harrison Barker, Cathleen Rickard, Kathryn Gualtieri,
and
Signe Nelson

In Memoriam

Rick Rescorla,
fellow writer and champion of the human spirit

Acknowledgments

For continual inspiration and influence, the author thanks Professor Lin Yun, Feng Shui master and spiritual leader of the Black Sect Tantric Buddhist Feng Shui School, and Grace Jagchid for friendship and the memorable tour of the Yun Lin Temple in Berkeley, California. Special thanks to Cathleen Rickard, friend, mentor, and owner/practitioner of Feng Shui Wisdom, in Kamuela, Hawaii, and to Feng Shui practitioner Gabrielle Alizay (*www.homepeace.com*) for an incredible phone consultation. For his charm, encouragement, and support of the mysteries, additional thanks go to Feng Shui practitioner/author Dennis Fairchild. The author is grateful to Madhu Brodkey, owner/consultant of Feng Shui Reflections, for sharing her knowledge.

Kudos to my agent Don Gastwirth for loyalty and perseverance. Without his efforts, The Feng Shui Mysteries would not have found such a fine home at Berkley Prime Crime. Sincere thanks to the exemplary publishing staff at Berkley Prime Crime and especially to my editor, Samantha Mandor, for her insights, and to Tom Colgan. All deserve medals for keeping up the work in the worst of times.

Every month the Capitola Women of Mystery meet to discuss books. The author is lucky to be a part of this lively, eclectic group and has gained much from their wit, observations, and generosity.

The following people have contributed to the work in special ways, some by answering a variety of questions, others providing creative insights, and some by allowing the author to Feng Shui their homes: David Davis, Jane Davis, Kevin Bransfield, Charlotte Morrison, Marilyn Hicks Fitzgerald, Mike Fitzgerald, and Bev and Gary Dart.

Deepest gratitude goes out to family and friends who provide the necessary support, enthusiasm, and encouragement no author can do without: Alberta Barker, Harrison Barker, Diane Barker, Dana Richmond, Signe Nelson, Lorraine Kessler, Dolores Osborne, Steve Osborne, Judy Osborne, Philip Osborne, Beverly Hogg, Harriet Manclark, John Manclark, Ava Dianne Day, Mara Wallis, Richard Recker, Sue Marshall, Donna Canfield, and for the coconut cakes, Sue Porter.

With extraordinary patience, Chris Osborne always lends his computer skills to each project and generously designed the author's home on the web: *www.deniseosbornemysteries.com*.

While this book is a work of fiction and all characters creations of an active imagination, all material concerning the practice of Feng Shui is, to the best of the author's knowledge, factual.

If you want to discover your subconscious dreams fears and beliefs, just look around your own home. You will find them represented in every nook and cranny.

—Denise Linn
Feng Shui for the Soul

THE BAGUA

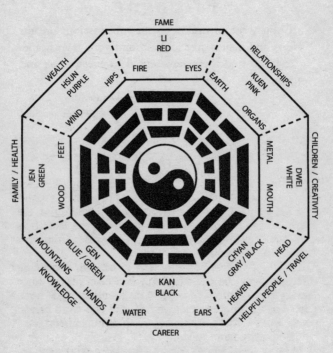

FAME
LI
RED
FIRE · EYES

RELATIONSHIPS
KUEN
PINK
EARTH
ORGANS

WEALTH
HSUN
PURPLE
WIND · HIPS
FEET

CHILDREN / CREATIVITY
DWEI
WHITE
METAL
MOUTH

FAMILY / HEALTH
JEN
GREEN
WOOD · FEET

GEN
BLUE / GREEN
MOUNTAINS · HANDS

KNOWLEDGE

KAN
BLACK
WATER · EARS
CAREER

CHYAN
GRAY / BLACK
HEAVEN
HEAD
HELPFUL PEOPLE / TRAVEL

◄ THE MOUTH OF CH'I ►

Prologue

"BIG house!" Gigi Gray shrieked from the backseat, her shrill child's voice ringing like a bell in her father's ears.

"Good eye, Gigi girl," John Gray said. A quick glance to his right confirmed his five-year-old daughter's sighting. Set far back from the road at the top of the rise, the old Victorian farmhouse blazed golden in the late afternoon sun, the buildings below the house hidden from view by tall hedges hugging the road.

The child's game of being first to call out something different along the coast highway had been played since leaving Santa Cruz. The boys, their attention to the west, described the rural seascape in one- and two-word bursts: ocean, waves, rocks, cliffs, big trees, farm, and surfers.

"How many more miles?"

"Almost there, Scotty," John announced with some relief, already slowing down. "Make sure your brother's coat is zipped tight. It's chilly outside."

He flipped on his right indicator as they passed a narrow road, bordered on either side by immensely tall eucalyptus. The road led up to the "Big House" and Ashcroft Farms, a thriving dairy, in the valley beyond.

"Punkins!" Gigi shouted. "Punkins!"

"It's *pumpkin* and you only get to say it once," Scotty, ever mindful of the rules, lectured his younger sister.

John pulled up close to the whitewashed stand set to one side of the three-acre patch, glad to see that there were still carved jack-o'-lanterns available. For good reason he'd been concerned that none would be left. The fellow who carved them did a great job, each one different. John's wife, a third grade teacher, had been so impressed with the one he'd bought yesterday, she'd taken it to the school today and sent John back for two more. The excursion also served to give her some quiet time while she decorated the house for Halloween. Normally, they would have just picked up a pumpkin from the grocery store and gone through the mess of carving it. But yesterday John had had business in Half Moon Bay. On the way up, the sight of hundreds of bright orange gourds, sweeping up from the road to a stand of pines, had cheered a drab drizzly day. On the return trip he'd stopped. The guy manning the stand had been closing up and with little effort talked John into buying one of his beautifully carved jack-o'-lanterns instead of an ordinary pumpkin. If he'd had a camera, John would have taken a picture of the guy holding his creation—he being something of an attraction himself. He was outfitted to look like one of the dozen or so scarecrows staked around the patch: Straw poked out from the neck and sleeves of his flannel shirt and out of the bottoms of his bib overalls. He'd been wearing a burlap mask with holes cut out to accommodate his eyes, nose, and mouth. As John approached, the man pulled off the mask and wiped his face with a red bandana.

Though he looked to be in his early thirties, he sported a hefty un-scarecrow-like waistline more common to middle-aged men. For someone who'd been out in the damp cold all day, he had a good disposition, one that apparently hadn't come from a bottle. Inside the stand, John had spied a plastic grocery bag full of empty soft drink cans and crushed HoHo and Twinkie wrappers. Had there been any evidence of alcohol, John certainly wouldn't have brought the children along.

Gigi, Scotty, and Kevin tumbled out of the car and dashed into the vast sea of pumpkins. John walked up to the stand, barking an order for them to stay away from the road.

From the row of jack-o'-lanterns displayed, John mentally chose two and pulled out his wallet. "Hello?"

There was no answer and no one was visible in the stand. *Maybe the guy went up to the trees to take a leak,* John mused. He carried the two jack-o'-lanterns to the car and set them on the hood.

"Hello? Anybody here?" he called again. He walked behind the stand where a pickup truck was parked. Thinking the guy might be taking a nap, John peered in the driver's-side window. No one was inside the cab or stretched out in the truck bed.

Standing between the truck and the stand, John looked around, biting the inside of his lip. The two boys were trying to lift a gourd that probably weighed more than both of them. Gigi crawled up on something behind a bale of straw.

John walked back to the front of the stand. Inside, a gutted pumpkin sat on a card table, one eye carved out. A green plastic lawn chair was pushed away from the table. The way things were situated, it appeared that the guy had left the stand momentarily, confirming John's first thought that he'd gone to the trees for privacy.

He tapped the wallet against his thigh, trying to decide between leaving money and waiting for the guy to return. Then he heard the boys arguing.

"Hey! You two cut it out or it's back in the car for both of you."

Kevin, the youngest, pulled away from his brother's grip and ran screaming to John. "He pushed me!"

"Did not! He fell down."

"That's it. Into the car," John said, sweeping the running boy into his arms. "Scotty, you too."

"Daaa-d!" Scotty whined. "We only just got here!"

"Look, Daddy," Gigi called out. She began jumping up and down on her perch. A loud farting noise could be heard, then another. Kevin squirmed and kicked in John's arms. John set him down and slipped his wallet into his back pocket. Five minutes, he told himself, and we're off.

Gigi jumped again, and the comical sound came again. The children began to choke with laughter.

"Gigi's making whiffies!" Scotty declared, and ran over to her.

"Am not!" Then she stopped and covered her mouth and nose with her small hands. "P.U.!" She jumped off the mound. She looked down at the ground then back at John. "Come see, Daddy."

"What is it, honey?"

Scotty answered first. "It's a scarecrow."

Then Gigi said, "And it's got real hands."

John began to run.

Chapter 1

"ABSOLUTELY not, Phyllis. Shame on you for asking." Salome Waterhouse's eyes didn't leave her reflection in the dressing room mirror as she fashioned her waist-length black hair into a figure eight at the back of her head—a real workout for her upper arms.

Leaning in the doorway, arms crossed at her chest, Phyllis Waterhouse continued to watch her cousin prepare for the evening, not a flicker of shame heating her cool blue eyes. "And you never tear the 'Do Not Remove' tags from mattresses, never toss 'Keep This Coupon' tickets, never sail through a stop sign. And you certainly never use the 'F' word."

"Oh please! Those wanting to find fault with feng shui would just love to hear about a practitioner who studied a property under false pretenses."

"You'll be looking around anyway."

"No, Phyl, I'll be conducting workshops."

"With your eyes closed?"

Salome turned to her cousin. A bright flush spread upward from the V-neck top of her silky long underwear. "Spying would be the worst kind of abuse of feng shui— which you're contemptuous of anyway."

"I respect feng shui."

"Enough to finally admit that the fish tank I gave you might have had something to do with your promotion to police chief?"

"Based on the recommendation of nine goldfish?"

"The energy opened up, Phyl, stimulating career opportunities."

Salome moved into the cedar-lined closet. She stepped into a black ankle-length gown that had a high Mandarin collar; long, tight sleeves; deep pockets; and a full skirt. She picked up a pair of soft black walking shoes but would wait to slip them on, as shoes were not worn in the house. While securing the frogs angled from neck to waist, she reentered the dressing room.

"You always look like you're ready to give the last rites when you wear that."

Even when asking a favor, Phyllis couldn't resist making a snide comment. Inured for the most part, Salome ignored the remark and checked her hair one last time, picked up a bag of toiletries and makeup, and swept past Phyllis into the bedroom.

Altering her strategy—flattery might be a straighter path to getting what she wanted—Phyllis turned around and followed Salome into the bedroom. "At the same time, you could pass for some Asian goddess."

Salome shot her a suspicious look then placed her toilet bag in a carryall beside a hanging bag lying open on the bed. She knew that Chinese-style clothes enhanced the Asian features she had inherited from her Japanese American mother. But being a middle-aged woman, albeit one with good bones, no gray hair yet, and a satisfactory figure—goddess was over the top. What was Phyllis up to?

Phyllis nodded toward the luminous image painted onto a ten-foot-long scroll hanging on the wall by the door, the bottom anchored by two porcelain balls with sapphire satin tassels. "Not like her, of course."

"Kwan Yin, Phyllis. Not *her*. The Chinese goddess of mercy and compassion."

Phyllis looked around the room for a moment, then moved to the bed and ran her hand across the pink silk quilt. "If memory serves, this area of the room represents relationships, right?"

"Right," Salome answered. Satisfied she'd packed all the right clothes for the weekend, Salome zipped up the bag.

"And pink. Now that's the color feng shui assigns to relationships."

"Right again." Salome flipped the bag over and checked the side pocket. "Underwear," she muttered and went back to the cedar-lined closet, pulling silky items and socks from the built-in drawers.

"A real bed, Salome!" Phyllis called out. "First time since you've lived in this house that you've had a bed. It's certainly an improvement on that futon rolled out on the floor. Even a nice rug to replace those grass whatcha-macallits."

"Tatami mats," Salome said, reentering the bedroom.

"That painting over there—" Phyllis pointed to a watercolor of two people walking hand in hand on an otherwise empty beach. "Another aspect of bedroom feng shui . . . accessorize in pairs. Of course, if I were a practitioner, I'd suggest you put that scroll in another room. Leads me to believe that the person who sleeps in this room still has an independent attitude—isn't willing to totally commit."

Salome began neatly packing the underwear in the hanging bag's side pocket.

"No mirrors," Phyllis went on. "Now that doesn't tell me, one way or the other, if kinky sex is on the program. Mirrors in the bedroom are verboten. Especially facing the bed. If the sleeper wakes up in the middle of the night, seeing her image will startle her. Over time this can lead to physical complaints." Phyllis bent down and, lifting the duvet, peeked under the bed. "Excellent! No dirty underwear, and you're not using the space for general storage. Allows the ch'i, the good energy, to flow freely."

"You've been doing your homework while I've been away," Salome conceded, though her impassive expression yielded no sign she was impressed.

"Finally, everything is new. Even smells new! Salome Waterhouse has finally decided to spice up the winter months she spends here in Holyrood-by-the-Sea. Next question, of course, is who's the lucky guy? Or should I say, intended victim? You haven't been back long enough for me to figure that one out. Though I can make an educated guess."

Salome rolled her wrist to check her watch, one with an enamel tai chi, or yin yang, symbol on the timepiece. "I'd best be going." She grabbed the hanging bag.

"Let me get the carryall," Phyllis offered.

Salome switched off the light and, with Phyllis at her heels, walked briskly along the wall separating the rooms on the west side from the open expanse of living room. Phyllis no longer noted the environment to assess her cousin. But this part of the house remained the same. Salome had only returned two weeks ago from her home in the Georgetown section of Washington, D.C., where she spent the other half of the year. Lately, she'd been in Holyrood only on weekends, the weekdays spent in San Diego, working on a series of feng shui videos with her mentor, Madame Wu. The past week had been hectic as they finished up. She flew home this morning. And after the weekend, she looked forward to settling in for the winter.

Before leaving Holyrood the previous March, Salome had suggested that Phyllis move the furnishings in her house "to stimulate the stagnant ch'i." Doing so had been much harder than Phyllis expected. She hadn't moved her couch in a dozen years. But gradually, she got into it, discovering in the process items she didn't even like and gave away. The house began to feel different, and she herself began to feel lighter, freer. That's when she met Gordon Child, a homicide detective up the coast in Santa Cruz and the reason she had left the station early to drop in on Salome before she headed out for the weekend. And she had to admit that the twenty-gallon tank and nine veil tail goldfish Salome had given her several years ago did improve the ambience in the living room, though she didn't quite believe it had anything to do with her subsequent promotion.

Leaving the luggage in the foyer, the two women went into the kitchen. Phyllis checked the locks on the windows, while Salome saw to the needs of her black and white kitty, ShiShi.

"You know don't you that some of the instructors begged off," Phyllis said, as Salome filled a lovely Imari bowl with dry cat food.

"Why would they do that?" Salome frowned. She filled another Imari bowl with bottled water. Named for the Japanese Guardian Lion, ShiShi deserved the best. Living up to his namesake, he had big paws to fill. And ShiShi did so with grace and much forbearance of human foibles.

"Jesus, Salome, why do you think? Toby Ashcroft's murder ring a bell?"

Salome set the fresh food and water on a clean red tray, which she placed on the floor, then stooped down to make sure the small kitty entrance at the base of the kitchen door swung freely. Like her, ShiShi had two homes. If for some reason he couldn't get into her house, he'd simply trot back to Otter Haven Resort just three blocks away, where he also lived with Salome's mother and father.

Salome straightened and checked the locks on the door. "That was what? Around Halloween?"

"Don't play coy with me. Of course you know when it happened. You'd just flown in from D.C."

"The police released the property, Phyl. But it surprises me that any of the instructors would cancel."

"Enlightened New Agers, my ass. Bunch of wussies if you ask me." Then she smiled. "But I suppose not everyone is as comfortable with the dark side as you are."

Salome moved into the living room and drew the drapes

across the floor-to-ceiling window and sliding door, closing off the magnificent view from her cliff side yard to Monterey Bay.

"Hell, I'd actually considered going myself."

"To learn or to snoop?" Salome tried to imagine Phyllis at the Star Institute. What came to mind was a Rottweiler let loose at a cat show.

"To snoop, of course. Too expensive, though. Christ the money people spend to find inner peace. In most cases, fifty cents for a chocolate bar would do the trick."

Finding a momentary quiet place inside herself, Salome straightened each of the nine red tassels positioned along the top of the drapes. This area of the house represented fame and/or one's reputation. Given the fact that she was going off to spend the weekend on display, leading feng shui workshops, she would have to be mindful of her every move. She would have preferred to take time for a proper ritual, but that would require chanting, and at the moment she didn't feel like giving Phyllis a performance. An internal confirmation of her good intentions would have to do.

"Anyway," Phyl went on, and considering what she said, it was synchronistic, blending smoothly into Salome's concerns with fame and reputation, "without the extra competition, you'll probably be the center of attention, your workshops SRO. That is if lots of attendees didn't cancel as well."

"I think the fees are nonrefundable," Salome noted.

"How enlightened."

Back in the foyer, Salome pulled her oilskin coat, an Australian Drizabone, from the closet. Storms were expected to hit the coast this weekend, starting late tonight.

"Here," Phyllis said, reaching for the coat, "let me help you with that."

"Too restrictive to wear while driving." Salome placed the coat on top of the bags. "But you could help by putting everything in the truck for me while I finish up."

Phyllis stiffened momentarily then did as asked. She

wasn't used to performing small tasks for others. Usually it was the other way around. Time was running out, and it appeared she was going to have to resort to confession. Salome had a soft heart. Besides, from all appearances, she too intended to bring her love life back from the dead.

Salome checked the windows in the study, made certain her answering machine tape was rewound, and closed the shutters in the adjoining "den," where she liked to curl up in the giant-size Poet's chair and read.

"All packed and ready to roll," Phyl said, addressing her reflection in the mirror above the Korean chest.

"Thanks, Phyl." Salome moved toward the door.

"Wait a sec."

"What?"

"Look, I've been seeing a guy."

"Hey! That's great. Anyone I—"

Before Salome could finish, Phyllis blurted, "He's the lead detective on the Ashcroft murder case."

Salome stopped. "Oh. I see."

"No, you probably don't. It's not what you're thinking—that I want to pass on information to impress him. That's not it."

"Then what is it?"

"I genuinely want to help him out. We're well beyond the impressing-each-other stage."

"So this is serious."

In a rare display of vulnerability, Phyllis blushed. Angry now at her body's betrayal, she became defensive.

The atmosphere in the foyer darkened and started to cloud, not unlike what was happening outside. Her features sharpened, and Salome was reminded of how much Phyllis resembled their late grandfather, Joshua Waterhouse, family patriarch and founding father of this small coastal village.

Phyllis took a breath and resumed. "He's retiring at the end of the year and planning to go into politics."

"Really? Is he going to run for city council or mayor?"

"Try governor of California."

"Yikes!" Salome had a fleeting vision of Phyllis storming through the Governor's Mansion in Sacramento.

"Yeah, well, two weeks and nary a clue. It would be easy to go along with the general consensus that Ashcroft was simply the victim of a passing motorist. A nasty one, for sure. But Gordon thinks there's more to it. One way or another, it would do him a lot of good if he caught the perp and put him away. He'll be remembered for his last case."

"And if he solves her brother's murder, Ivy Ashcroft might be willing to make a substantial campaign contribution?"

Phyllis didn't comment, her stare statement enough.

"Oh all right," Salome said with a sigh. "But don't be counting on me, Phyllis. I'll be busy. If I happen upon something," she paused, "I'll tell you about it. But don't you tell him that I'm doing this for you—though it wouldn't take a rocket scientist to figure out your source."

"Trust me, I'll keep you out of it."

They traded in the slippers, extra pairs provided in a basket by the door, for their regular walking shoes and exited the house.

The little blue Toyota pickup, packed earlier with her show-and-tell feng shui paraphernalia, was parked on the drive in front of the cottage. Salome climbed behind the wheel.

Phyllis pulled a manila folder out of her shoulder bag and knocked on the driver's-side window.

Salome rolled the window down. Phyllis passed her the folder.

"Just a review of the case. Might give you some ideas about where to look."

Phyl bent down and squeezed Salome's shoulder. "Stay out of trouble."

"You never know. I might get the urge to run around ripping tags off mattresses."

Chapter 2

WHAT Phyllis didn't know was that Salome did indeed plan on looking around the Star Institute with more than just simple curiosity. She'd begun a private study of properties where murder had been committed, her purpose being to see if similarities existed that hinted at potential violence. She needed to study many more properties before drawing any conclusions, but when she did she planned to publish the findings and hopefully interest law enforcement. Certainly it would be a hard sell but already feng shui was being recognized as beneficial in the work environment. Through the grapevine, she'd heard that police in Burbank, California, had brought in a feng shui practitioner to make recommendations on relieving stress so common to the job. To take it from the office into the field, however, was a different matter altogether.

As a practitioner, she knew that lifestyle revealed character. In the case of murder victims, environmental clues could suggest suspects. Just as Phyllis had pointed out in the bedroom—factoring in, of course, prior knowledge which was itself important—Salome did intend to change her solitary lifestyle in Holyrood. If Salome were to become a murder victim, whoever investigated would be wise to suspect either a lover or potential lover. However, if the investigator didn't know she'd spent the previous six years sleeping on a single futon on the floor, he wouldn't be aware of how great a change Salome had made. Without knowledge of feng shui, he would not be aware of how much care she'd taken in the bedroom. He'd see a bed but not a bed carefully placed in the proper position. He'd see pink and assume it was a normal feminine color, unaware of the greater significance. Pink represented the pure joy and happiness achieved by love, the very reason it was the color associated with the relationship gua. The watercolor of the couple he would presume to be a romantic touch, not knowing that it stimulated active seeking of a mate.

On the other hand, if he were to see pictures and paintings of single individuals in the bedroom, he might be wrong to assume that she was actively looking for a partner. Keeping her Kwan Yin scroll in the bedroom—the solitary figure dominating the room—led Salome herself to wonder if she truly wanted to commit to a relationship—as Phyllis had pointed out. In the bedroom of a couple, pictures/photographs of single individuals suggest that one of them is not completely into the relationship. For in the shared bedroom, decorative items should be in pairs.

Salome believed feng shui practitioners were excellent investigators, able to recognize the overlooked details that could expedite criminal investigations. To reject feng shui out of hand was to foolishly disregard a powerful resource. But egos and self-image too often stood in the way. If she were Phyllis, she'd consult—

Suddenly she realized that that was exactly what Phyllis was doing. In her own backhanded, backdoor way, Phyllis was consulting Salome on the Ashcroft murder investigation. Salome felt a wave of triumph. Of course, if confronted with the fact, Phyllis would doubtless deny it. But there it was. And if her observations did help bag a killer, she wouldn't really be *studying a property under false pretenses*, to paraphrase her earlier protest. Not totally, anyway, considering that she'd planned on looking around for her private feng shui study.

After about forty minutes of frustrating stop-and-go Friday evening traffic, her tension eased as she left the city and entered the less-congested stretch of Highway 1. Just off to the left was a rugged coastline and rough waters more popular with surfers than beachgoers. Here the squalls hadn't waited, and wind pushed the rain across the roadway and onto the rolling hills to the east. There were no lights along the road except those in the occasional farmhouse and, of course, the headlights of passing motorists, streaky and uneven in the rain.

Once settled in to the drive, though fully alert to traffic, weather, and road dips and twists—particularly treacherous on the two-lane stretches—Salome allowed a part of her brain to order the bits and pieces she knew of the Ashcroft murder.

Tobias "Toby" Ashcroft's body had been found in the pumpkin patch, a section of the Ashcroft estate just off the highway. His throat had been slit and he'd bled to death. In keeping with the spirit of Halloween, each day he went out to sell pumpkins, he dressed up like a scarecrow. Actual scarecrows, perhaps a dozen, decorated the patch, which is why his moldering corpse had first been mistaken for one that had fallen beside a bale of hay. The county coroner had estimated the time between his death and when his body was found to be somewhere in the neighborhood of sixteen to eighteen hours.

Salome recalled visiting the same pumpkin patch when she was a child. Her mother would pile the four daughters and Phyllis into the old station wagon, her father would take the Ford pickup, and the little caravan would drive up the coast, where they'd load up the bed of the truck with pumpkins to decorate Otter Haven Resort. Back then, no one bothered to add scarecrows, and, from a child's perspective, the patch had looked like mile upon unbroken mile of assorted orange globes—big ones, little ones, *huge* ones in every shade from deep red-orange called *La Rouge* to pumpkins that were actually white.

Salome thought she'd like someone like Toby Ashcroft, who went to the trouble to decorate the patch—and himself. Making the effort to fashion the pumpkins into jack-o'-lanterns further indicated a childlike spirit. But of course, that wasn't too surprising, given his dot com business, which, before the tech industry "crash," earned him a fortune: Toys for Techies. John Gray, the man who found Ashcroft's body, had been astonished when he learned that Toby Ashcroft wasn't just a farmhand with an artistic flair when it came to pumpkins.

A sign posted on the side of the road indicated that the speed limit had dropped to 45 mph. The road turned abruptly to the left and a little farther on dipped steeply. At the bottom, Salome downshifted. At the top were the lights of the tiny hamlet of Davenport. Farther inland would be Bonnie Doon Farms, famous for their fragrant soaps and lotions and luxuriant fields of lavender.

In barely a moment, the terrain darkened again. Railroad tracks meandered off to the right, and Salome figured she had less than ten miles to go.

Her thoughts had just turned back to Toby Ashcroft, when the cab suddenly filled with light. She glanced into the rearview mirror. A motorist had come up on her tail. She maintained her speed. Not too far ahead would be one of the passing lanes provided every few miles.

The storm intensified, and she flicked her wipers to their highest speed. Whoever was behind her didn't seem to notice the heavier rain and would not budge. Several cars sped by on the left. Salome looked right for a turnoff but couldn't see much of anything.

Behind her, the driver began flashing his headlights. The driver's impatience annoyed her, then actually seemed to enter the cab. Salome swallowed nervously. She would have grabbed her bottle of water but didn't want to take her hands from the wheel. Then she wondered if something was wrong with the back end of the truck. Maybe the driver was flashing a warning. But everything felt normal; no shimmying to suggest a flat.

Up ahead there were no lights indicating oncoming traffic. She inched over to the right so the jerk behind her could see. The driver swerved left, filling her side mirror with blinding light.

Salome pulled over even farther, and the other driver shot up beside her. She ventured a quick look. A man was behind the wheel, his face tinted red in the dashboard lights. He was looking at her, his face contorted in rage. He seemed to be yelling. For an instant she thought she recognized him, but then she saw the oncoming car, a dark shadow that had come out of nowhere.

Salome jerked the wheel to the right. She heard the wail of a horn, and then the cacophonous bray of another. The truck bounced hard, then began bobbling to the left and right. Her body strained against the seat belt. Something black and massive loomed just ahead. Her right hand had somehow left the wheel and gripped the gearshift knob. She pressed in the clutch, downshifted to second, and hit the brakes. Amazingly, the truck was still running when she abruptly stopped. Maybe ten seconds had passed since she spotted the oncoming car that had no lights, probably someone who had just turned off one of the farm roads.

Her head fell back against the headrest, and she took a moment to let her heartbeat slow down. Several cars passed, evidence that there hadn't been an accident. But of course she would have heard the impact. No one stopped, so the truck probably looked okay.

For the moment, a punctual arrival at the presentation dinner didn't matter. She needed to get out and check the truck, but before doing so, she wanted to recount every detail of those intense few seconds. Her life might depend on it. Maybe her imagination had played tricks, but she couldn't shake the fact that the driver looked uncannily like a recently made enemy, Duncan Mah. Had he followed her from Washington, D.C.? Was it coincidence, even synchronistic, that they'd met up on this isolated road three thousand miles from the mansion beside the Potomac River where she'd last seen him? But even her concept of synchronicity didn't stretch that far. She remembered the blood on the back of his head caused by the paperweight she'd thrown at him, remembered the hot feel of his hatred. Her ex-husband's warning was still as clear as it had been six months ago: *"I bet he'll pop up again. He's not likely to forget you any time soon, Mei. From now on you better watch your back."*

The vehicle was a gold Lexus, of that she was certain. Mah had money and would likely be driving an expensive car. And he'd moved to Washington from San Francisco.

"Good God," she muttered. For Mah to be around here wasn't really that odd.

Light from a passing car hit the ten-millimeter faceted crystal that was hanging on a nine-inch red cord from her rearview mirror. For a few seconds the windshield was covered in tiny rainbows of color. Salome reached up and touched the crystal. Some might say its presence had no protective value whatsoever. But she believed otherwise. That she and others on the road had not become statistics provided proof to her.

She thanked whatever deities were watching the road and took several deep breaths. Leaving the engine running, she set the parking brake, unbuckled the seat belt, took a flashlight from the glove compartment, and slipped on the Drizabone.

Outside, the overhanging branches of an old cypress tree shielded her from the full force of the storm as she dashed around the truck. She kept an eye on the road, alert to the possible return of the gold Lexus.

The front left fender lightly kissed the thick and solid trunk of the cypress. There wasn't even room to slip her little finger between them. She shuddered to think what might have happened.

The right front tire had dug into the muddy shoulder,

but with careful maneuvering she could avoid getting stuck. Otherwise, the truck looked okay.

Back in the cab, she pulled a towel from behind the driver's seat and mopped her wet head and face. She checked her watch: she'd be late for the seven o'clock start. At least she didn't have far to go, but this was not the kind of start she'd envisioned for a weekend advertised as "Enlightenment for the Discriminating New Ager." She eased back onto the road.

A short time later, Salome spotted the freshly painted sign that displayed an arrow pointing to the right: Welcome to the Star Institute. She turned into the narrow road embraced on each side by towering eucalyptus trees, their tops hidden in the low ceiling.

The road went on and on without any breaks in the trees. She wondered if she'd missed a turn and should back up. The trees grew so close together she couldn't see much of anything to the right or left. Finally, her lights shone on another new-looking sign, this one less friendly: Parking for Star Institute Only. All Others Will Be Towed.

Making the left turn, she crossed a little bridge. On the other side, yet another sign directed her to "Instructors' Parking," a long row of covered spaces. She passed half a dozen cars or so and pulled into the next available space. Now the anxiety of being late set in, and she hoped the presentations were by name, not subject, and in alphabetical order. But maybe such order wasn't considered enlightened, which reminded her of how little she really knew about the Star Institute, other than that the co-owner and brother of Ivy Ashcroft had been murdered two weeks ago. A month ago she'd been invited to replace another feng shui practitioner who'd been originally scheduled and for some reason could not attend. Not being the first choice didn't bother her; branching out into public speaking was an aspect of her career that was still in its infancy. Practitioners who had published books were usually first choice.

She plucked the carryall, her satchel, which held her speech among other things, and an umbrella from the backseat. Later, when she had her room assignment, she'd come back for everything else.

One yellow bulb lighted the parking area and not very effectively, creating more shadows than illumination. The leaves rustling in the wind added to the spooky atmosphere. Salome patted her pocket, assuring herself she still had her flashlight.

After making sure the car was locked, Salome hurried to the end of the sheltered parking. She paused for a moment to look around and get her bearings. The ocean wasn't far, just on the other side of the highway. She could hear the waves crashing against rocks and cliffs and smell the sharp brine mixed with the tangy scent of eucalyptus.

Behind the Instructors' Parking was General Parking, unsheltered. Quite a few cars were scattered around the large, open lot, light provided by a single, ordinary streetlight in the center. She saw no one and felt eerily alone, like she'd stumbled onto an abandoned movie set and the cars were only props, not really owned by anyone.

Heightening the gloomy sensation was the fact that a man had been murdered just a few hundreds yards away. An unwelcome vision of lifeless eyes in the holes of a burlap scarecrow mask appeared, quickly joined by the driver's red-tinted face engorged by rage. Duncan Mah?

She shook her head to clear it and adjusted her bags so she could carry both the umbrella and flashlight. Without wasting any more time, she plunged into the dark wet night, unable to shake the thought that the fearful encounter on the road heralded the beginning of a very long weekend.

Chapter 3

PUSHED by the wind, Salome shot through a pair of glass doors. Feeling like a piece of flotsam, the umbrella inside out, Salome took a moment to catch her breath just inside a quiet, spacious rotunda. Light shone from globes embedded in the high ceiling, the subdued illumination lending a sense of calm. Two wooden benches on either side of the doors provided the only seating. Straight ahead was a large circular desk where a figure in a white hooded cloak stood in profile speaking into a phone.

Little puddles glistened on the polished black granite, some leading to the desk, others veering off toward corridors to the right and left. Behind the desk rose a pair of red padded doors.

Salome scurried up to the desk. The hooded figure put down the phone and picked up a clipboard.

"The evening's program has been somewhat abbreviated," came a familiar voice in what sounded like a mantra. "Your name?"

"Barbara?" Salome said, thinking the white-robed individual to be her neighbor Barbara Boatwright. But Barbara was the last person she'd expect at a place like the Star Institute. Not that Barbara wasn't enlightened—or a pursuant of enlightenment—it was simply that she had never shown interest in New Age subjects, and, in the past, even dismissed feng shui as hocus-pocus.

"Salome! God, what a messy night." Barbara pulled back the hood, revealing soft ash blonde curls, gold hoop earrings, and perfect makeup. She looked to be in her late thirties; since Salome had last seen her, she had shaved off twenty years.

"You look wonderful, Barbara! But what are you doing here?"

Barbara shrugged. "Billie Ruth talked me into coming. Ivy enlisted my help when someone didn't show up to greet people." Barbara checked a jeweled gold watch then the clipboard. "We'll have to talk later. Cryogenics should just be finishing up. Chaos theory canceled—could have used him tonight," Barbara added, with a slight smile on lips fuller than Salome remembered. Had Barbara had a face-lift, a collagen treatment?

"There's a bathroom right over there," she nodded to her right. "I think you'd better freshen up."

"I guess I look pretty frightful."

"Very wild wiccan. Which is okay, I have nothing against wiccans. It's just that people will be expecting a tidier look from a feng shui person."

"Right."

"I'll let Ivy know you're here." Barbara picked up a walkie-talkie. "She'll be introducing you." She concluded with a dismissive wave of her fine-boned artistic hand, "Now off you go. And be quick."

In the bathroom Salome pulled off her coat, cleaned the mud and grass from the hem of her skirt and shoes. Her hair was a disaster. She pulled out the remaining pins and gave it a quick swipe, letting it hang behind her back, half her thoughts on the radical change in Barbara; even the age spots on her hands were gone.

Back in the rotunda, Barbara handed over an aquamarine-colored folder. "This has all the information you need for the weekend, including room assignment, room key, and meal ticket. The auditorium is just through those red doors. You're sitting at table seven at the front and left of the stage. You can leave your coat and bags with me if you like. Might not be any room at your table."

"That would be great, Barbara. Thanks."

Barbara stashed the carryall and rain gear under a section of the desk. Salome kept her satchel.

"See you later," Salome said.

With a *whoosh*, the red padded doors closed behind her. Hurrying along the left wall, Salome noted that most of the tables were filled and all neatly set with lighted red candles, white table linen, silverware, water goblets, and standard white crockery. Dinner also appeared to be "abbreviated." Each table had baskets of crackers and rolls and platters of assorted fruits and vegetables. Up ahead she spotted a table against the wall set up with coffee and tea service. A hot cup of tea was just what she needed.

As she placed a cup beneath the spigot of the urn labeled "Hot Water," a woman in a black suit strode to the podium center stage. She shifted some papers, then began.

"Our next presenter is feng shui practitioner Salome Waterhouse, who will be hosting the feng shui workshops." The woman paused and looked out at the audience.

Salome raised her hand to make her presence known.

After a nod, Ivy Ashcroft continued. "Ms. Waterhouse apprenticed for five years with a master of what we in the West refer to as the Chinese art of placement and has been a professional practitioner for half a dozen years.

Salome carried the cup of hot water, a tea bag on the saucer, to table seven, the last in the front row, and slipped into an empty seat.

"Ms. Waterhouse is a local—" Ivy looked up for a moment now, apparently improvising, "I say local but actually she's bicoastal. And no, that's not a sexual designation."

If Ivy was after a laugh, she got it. Salome cringed

slightly, while pulling a folder from a pocket in her black leather satchel.

"She divides her time between Holyrood, just down the coast from us, and Washington, D.C. I think we could very well see some necessary improvements in this country if Salome applied her special skills on Capitol Hill, not to mention the White House!"

More laughter.

"Ladies and gentlemen, please welcome feng shui practitioner, Salome Waterhouse."

On the wave of applause, Salome rode up the side steps, taking the opportunity to examine her hostess, who remained at the podium, lightly clapping large masculine-looking hands. The action caused a large diamond to flash on the ring finger of her left hand. Having spoken to Ivy Ashcroft on the telephone to accept the E-mailed invitation, Salome found her appearance sharply contrasted to what she'd imagined. She'd expected someone small and delicate-featured to fit the soft, sweet voice. But Ivy was tall and oddly proportioned, as if body parts had been randomly selected: short, square torso, placed on wide hips; long, muscular legs attached to big feet (which did match the large hands). Straight shoulder-length brown hair partially hid a long, narrow neck, an unsubstantial pike on which to bear such a large head.

Heavy eyebrows added to the basiliscan intensity of her wide-spaced black eyes. Her nose was long and sharp, the nostrils high-arced and flaring, the total effect similar to a line drawing of a bird in flight. Beneath a long philtrum, her small, pert mouth formed a quick, cool smile. Ivy held out her hand, and Salome's much smaller version disappeared in the firm grip. "Glad to meet you," Ivy said in a low tone. Had she been otherwise, Salome figured all the bones in her hand would have been crushed.

"Try not to go over fifteen minutes. Remember, you're pitching your workshops not giving way any secrets. Since you missed the orientation meeting, I just wanted you to know the game plan."

Salome nodded. After pointing out bottles of water in the body of the podium, Ivy grabbed her notes, walked stage left, and stood in the shadows.

By now the applause had died. Salome smiled at the audience and squared the pages of her speech on the podium, taking a moment to orient herself. Though the words came easily and sometimes seemed to tumble out on their own, she liked to have a copy in front of her. After a deep breath and another smile, she began. "Feng shui literally means wind and water. And we have both in abundance tonight!

"Whether we accept it or not, like it or not, all of us are affected by the energy that surrounds us. So why not learn about what can be done to maximize the positive— that is, attract those things we desire and need the most— and minimize the negative? Do you want to stimulate your love life? Increase your wealth? Advance in your career? Improve relations with family members? Even learn how to control teenagers?"

The audience laughed, a few applauded—those were the ones she could count on to fill up space in her workshops. Controlling teenagers always attracted befuddled parents.

"For all the above and more, feng shui can help. Feng shui works. What I'll be doing is presenting effective, proven ways you can improve whatever life situation happens to be in need of change. What feng shui requires of you is a commitment to improving your environment. And, as I imagine many of you are already aware, this first requires basic cleaning and the removal of clutter."

Salome then held up an eight by ten copy of the octagonal template known as the Bagua. "Each of you should have one of these in your folders. If you'll look at them now, I'll give you a brief overview.

"This is called a Bagua. In Black Sect feng shui, which I practice, we use the Bagua to determine the location of life situations. Each section is called a gua. Though the shape is an octagon, we include the center, which represents harmony, so there are nine guas in all. What you do is superimpose the design over your property as a whole, then your house or apartment, then each room."

She pointed to the bottom of the page. "Now I want to direct your attention here, to the mouth of ch'i—ch'i being energy. The entrance to your property will be located at one of these three places. On the left you see knowledge and spirituality. In the middle is career. On the right, we have helpful people and travel.

"Imagine the front door to your residence at one of these three places. From that point you can easily determine the locations of the remaining life situations, which, as you can see are, moving clockwise from knowledge and spirituality: family and health, followed by wealth, then fame, then relationships, then children and creativity and, finally, helpful people and travel. In the workshops we'll cover all nine areas of the Bagua and I'll explain how you can use simple techniques—such as moving the furniture around or bringing a certain color into a room— to change any situation for the better."

After outlining what the audience could expect from her workshops, Salome concluded by saying, "Use the Bagua when you go to your rooms tonight. Check the position of your bed, and you'll see which life situation you are sleeping in. Have fun with it!"

Salome gave a slight bow and returned to her seat; the response to her presentation was mildly enthusiastic applause.

A number of people had entered while she'd been speaking, and two more chairs at her table were filled.

Salome quickly introduced herself to her tablemates. A stiff woman seated on Salome's right, her thick dark hair pulled tightly into French braids, introduced herself as Carla Whitmore. Earnestly and with a touch of condescension, she commented, "If you want to put feng shui to good use, you should direct your energies to domestic violence and help battered women."

"Actually, I support a women's shelter on the east coast."

"Feng shui is awesome!" announced a young woman seated opposite Salome who stood and extended her hand across the center of the table. "I'm Cherie."

Finally Salome came to the last person, an older gentleman on her left, outfitted in an attractive dark blue cashmere sweat suit, the message in white on the shirt reading: This Old Spouse.

"Harve Goldmark. I'll probably miss your workshops—I'm here for the yoga—but feng shui sounds interesting. Got a business card?"

Salome dug in her satchel for the special wallet. Adorning one side was a hand-beaded Bagua, each gua filled in with a different bright color. She handed Goldmark her card.

"That's pretty," he said, rubbing a finger on the Bagua.

"Come to my workshop, and you'll learn how to use it."

Without comment, he took the card.

"I'm on the west coast until March. But so you know, I do consultations over the phone. That requires a faxed or mailed floor plan . . ."

He held up his hand. "Excuse me, but here's my man."

Along with everyone else, Salome turned her attention to the stage, where Ivy introduced Roger Cane. Goldmark applauded with great relish. On her right, Carla Whitmore sat back in her seat and crossed her arms at her chest, making a statement by not clapping. She seemed to glow with open hostility. Salome wondered vaguely what Carla had against Cane.

A celebrity in yoga circles, Cane had appeared on *Oprah* and many national and local talk shows promoting his books and workshops using yoga as sex therapy. He was tall and loose-limbed like an endurance swimmer. His dark hair was close-cropped, like a shadow on his well-formed skull. Over a skin-tight white body stocking, he wore flowing light blue silk pants that clung to the bulges when he moved. And move he did, from one side of the stage to the other, while delivering his presentation. He started with a bang.

"Copulation is merely the final act in a complex series of actions that most of us in the West are unaware of. But that unawareness has been purposely ingrained—we've been trained to shut down our senses. Just look at babies. They're busy awakening themselves to everything. Their bodies are bundles of sensations. When you were a baby that was the last time you experienced the profound joy of your body. Your parents put that self-knowledge to sleep with their rules and taboos—passed down from their parents.

"We suffer from centuries of a hybrid I call Western Ignorance Conditioning. We're taught to believe that sex is primarily for procreation instead of being a normal and integral part of our daily life. Our bodies are reviled as conductors of sensual expression. And, of course, what has this done but turn us into the chattel of the church and state. The church needs worshipers—and that all-important tithing. The state needs soldiers to defend it and worker bees to maintain the economic order. With both state and church in control, you can bet they will strip you of your natural, your free sensual spirit. But they can't really—you're born with it. So they condition you into thinking it doesn't exist.

"In my workshops you will awaken and rediscover your sensual self. It's there, believe me, has just been sleeping for all but a few months of your life. Using simple techniques, you can attain whole body and mind sex. You'll learn the exquisite sensation of breathing your partner into you. As foreplay, it is matchless."

Finally he paused and looked around the audience. "Who here has experienced whole body sex?"

Salome turned to look around. Most people appeared slightly embarrassed but interested to see who, if anyone, would raise their hand. Then a slightly built man who hardly looked the type to elevate anyone's blood pressure, stood up.

"You, sir. Is whole body sex normal for you?"

"Absolutely. But I'd rather do it than talk about it." He pumped his fist then sat down.

Despite the self-promotion, Salome didn't see anyone running to get to the man's table. But the incident reminded her that this was her first time attending a mixed-topic weekend with a bunch of strangers. Particularly, a sex therapist like Roger Cane would attract more than his share of nuts and flakes. Salome wondered if Ivy simply accepted anyone who could pay the fee or if she conducted background checks.

The director of the Women's Study program at a state university and author of numerous books, Angela Platt, spoke next. "We are conditioned to believe that unmarried, middle-aged, and elderly women are one, lonely; two, past their prime and no longer useful—useful, inferring women's use—procreation . . ."

Harve Goldmark groaned. "Christ, not one of *them*." With a shake of his head, he left the table, returning to his seat when Platt finished.

Close to nine o'clock the presentations concluded. General consensus at the table was that Roger Cane's workshop would fill to capacity. Ivy made some final announcements.

"As I mentioned at the beginning of the program, we've had a few cancellations. A list of workshops no longer available will be posted at the front desk." Ivy cleared her throat. "Finally, in memory of my brother, Tobias Ashcroft, I'd like to conclude the evening with a song."

People began to look around in embarrassment, probably expecting a sing-along.

"Toby had very eclectic taste in music—as in all things—but this was his favorite."

Ivy nodded at someone in one of the front row tables. A man in his mid-thirties, and decked out like a Highlander in a red plaid kilt, joined Ivy at the podium. He had a Slavic-looking face, and as several people commented at her table, he bore a remarkable resemblance to a young, clean-shaven Stephen Wozniak, cofounder of Apple Computers. Of course, in Silicon Valley, a dynamo like Wozniak would be recognizable, especially to those working in the computer industry.

"That must be why he looks familiar to me," Salome commented to Harve Goldmark. But she couldn't shake a feeling that he was familiar for a different reason, which, at the moment, eluded her.

"To sing for us tonight is Toby's dear friend—"

Harve leaned in close and whispered, "Dear friend, my behind. I'll bet he lost millions."

Salome turned, her expression puzzled.

"In the dot com crash. He was one of Tobias Ashcroft's partners in Toys for Techies. Wouldn't surprise me if he did it. Might even have the very knife that slit young Toby's throat tucked away in that moth-eaten sporran he's wearing."

". . . 'The October Song,' written by Robin Williamson of The Incredible String Band," Ivy said.

While everyone applauded, Salome whispered, "I didn't get his name."

"Prenderville. Ross Prenderville."

In a clear, smooth baritone, though not one that would indicate a career as a singer, Prenderville sang. But after a moment, the quality of his voice didn't matter, the *emotion* expressed pushed the lyrics forward. It wasn't the medium so much as the message:

> I'll sing you this October song
> Oh, there is no song before it.
> The words and tune are none of my own,
> For my joys and sorrows bore it.
>
> Beside the sea
> The brambly briars in the still of evening,
> Birds fly out behind the sun
> And with them I'll be leaving.

The fallen leaves that jewel the ground,
They know the art of dying.
And leave with joy their glad gold hearts,
In the scarlet shadows lying.

When hunger calls my footsteps home,
The morning follows after,
I swim the seas within my mind,
And the pine-trees laugh green laughter.

I used to search for happiness,
And I used to follow pleasure,
But I found a door behind my mind,
And that's the greatest treasure.

For rulers like to lay down laws,
And rebels like to break them,
And the poor priests like to walk in chains,
And God likes to forsake them.

I met a man whose name was Time,
And he said, "I must be going,"
But just how long that was,
I have no way of knowing.

Sometimes I want to murder time
Sometimes when my heart's aching,
But mostly I just stroll along,
The path that he is taking.

When he finished, no one moved, not even Prenderville. Candlelight flickered, but there was no sound. Then, one or two people lightly applauded. More joined in. Someone whistled. Then suddenly the applause was thunderous. People began to stand, the ovation for the singer who had held them in his thrall, for the writer who had charmed them with his mystic vision.

Prenderville bowed, and without another word, he and Ivy left the stage. The applause continued until they reached table five, in the center and the second table from

Salome's. Prenderville sat with his back to the stage, Ivy to his right. From her seat, Salome could see him and Ivy. He picked up her hand and kissed it, then leaned forward to talk to someone across from him. The candlelight bathed his face in red. He laughed at something, momentarily distorting his features. Salome froze, instantly knowing why she'd found him familiar.

On the one hand, she felt relief that she hadn't had an encounter with Duncan Mah after all. No, the person driving the gold Lexus had been Ross Prenderville.

Chapter 4

☯

CURIOUS to see if Prenderville was mentioned possibly as a suspect, Salome wanted to settle into her room and read Phyllis's report on the Ashcroft murder. But as people began to leave or mingle, Salome spent a few minutes in polite conversation with those at her table. Both Cherie and another woman were interested in her workshops, and it would be rude to leave abruptly.

Ivy and Prenderville's table was mobbed. So was Roger Cane's.

When Salome's table emptied and the crowd around Ivy and Prenderville thinned, she got up and, carrying her satchel, went to table five.

"Quite a performance," she said to Prenderville, standing on the opposite side of the table so she wouldn't have to shake his hand.

"Thank you," he replied, giving her a clinical once-over: *female, middle-aged* . . . Next!

"Do you sing professionally?" she asked, wanting to give him an extra moment to recognize her.

"Oh no. Just for fun."

Ivy moved closer and took his arm. "Excellent presentation," Ivy said to Salome. "Wish I could take your workshop."

"Do you practice feng shui?"

She shook her head. "Feng shui was Toby's idea. When we decided to reopen the institute he thought about having a consultation. Then he decided to see how things went with the workshops. If he liked the practitioner, you as it turned out, he was going to ask you to feng shui the property."

"I still can."

Ivy gave Salome a tight smile then went on, "If you'll excuse us, Ms. Waterhouse, there's still a lot to do to get ready for tomorrow."

Since Prenderville had given no indication that he recognized her, she wondered if road rage was simply a part of his daily driving routine, the drivers he intimidated forgotten as soon as he forced them to the side of the road. If so, he was both arrogant and dangerous.

Making a quick exit proved difficult, as a number of people stopped her for a word, among them Barbara Boatwright and Billie Ruth.

Salome had known Billie Ruth since high school. Though "Ruth" was her surname, she'd always been called Billie Ruth, as though the two were hyphenated.

"Should be an interesting weekend, wouldn't you say?" Barbara began. "Hard to believe, but I used to come to retreats here back when the institute first opened in the late sixties and several times in the seventies. I was friends with the Ashcrofts—Bill and Alice—and have known Ivy and Toby since they were kids. The institute was competition for Esalen down in Big Sur, and believe me, I met some interesting people here."

Barbara smiled at Salome. "I'll bet your workshops will be packed, Salome."

"Don't count on it," Billie Ruth interjected, a challenge in her hard green eyes. "My money's on the yoga guy." She wore her hair cut short in a spiky do that suited her sharp features and personality. "But you can't help but

feel sorry for Angela Pratt. Maybe a couple little old ladies'll show up for her sessions, but that's about it."

"The name's Platt not Pratt, and I plan on taking her
workshops," Barbara snapped. "No offense, Salome."

"None taken." Salome well knew what Barbara thought
of feng shui.

Barbara continued, "In my humble opinion, Cane's just
exploiting common feelings of sexual inadequacy. But, I
suppose he is the resident celebrity. As for cryogenics—
well, I could care less about being frozen and waking up
in a hundred years in the same body."

"Come on, Barb, let's go see what Cane looks like up
close and personal."

Barbara rolled her eyes. Salome watched the two
women plow through the crowd toward the table where
Roger Cane was holding court. As she started to turn, she
noticed her tablemate, Carla Whitmore, standing a few
feet from Cane, glaring so intensely she could almost
imagine Cane's lithe body instantly turning to ash. No
doubt, Carla had a problem with the man. Once again, she
was reminded that these events could attract all kinds of
kooks. Not that anything was wrong with Carla; maybe
she had a legitimate beef with the guy. It was just that
Salome hadn't been particularly circumspect when accepting the invitation, blithely assuming that all involved
would be concerned only with self-improvement and
packing a positive, open attitude.

At the desk in the rotunda, she collected her rain gear
and carryall from a woman wearing a name tag that read:
Marcella Cruz. With her thick black hair, dark eyes, and
angular features, she looked Native American. She carried
herself with a certain amount of authority, giving Salome
the impression that she was the woman Barbara had been
filling in for.

Slipping on her coat, Salome pulled a map of the
grounds from the information packet. With the administration building in the center, there were three houses to
the north of it: Leary, Ram Dass, and Watts. On the south

side were Dilbert, Dogbert, and Tolkien. On Salome's map, Watts was circled in green.

"Let me help you," Marcella Cruz said and introduced herself.

"I'm Salome Waterhouse."

"Oh wow! The feng shui lady! Looks like you're in Watts House. As in Alan Watts. Has the best accommodations—private baths. And just so you know, the instructors aren't all in the same house. You'll have guests around you."

"That doesn't bother me."

"Good. We just don't want you to be hassled—that used to happen sometimes when really famous people came here—Alan Watts, Ram Dass, Timothy Leary, Ken Kesey—they were all friends of the Ashcrofts. Things were really different then, what with the partying going on. No alcohol or anything now. Not even meat."

Marcella leaned in close. Salome could smell lavender. "I think it was a lot more fun back then."

Marcella pulled an ordinary key from the packet. An attached tag read: Watts 4. "The key is to the room only. The front doors are always unlocked."

Handing over the key, she gave Salome a wistful smile. "Wish you'd been here a month ago."

"Why?"

"Toby might be alive. Maybe you could have discovered negative energy in the Big House."

"What's the Big House?"

"The Ashcroft family house. Up on the hill. It was built a long time ago, way before the institute—this all used to be pasture. That's where Toby lived. He had the downstairs. Ivy lives upstairs. Maybe his bed was in the wrong place."

"Well, possibly I'll be invited in for a consultation. In fact, I was just talking to Ivy about it."

Marcella's expression became skeptical. "I wouldn't count on it. Not the Big House. She won't let anyone in

any more. Threw a fit when the police had to look around.
But she couldn't keep them out."

Suddenly her face brightened. "Will you do my house?"

Salome didn't have the heart to simply say no or state
her fees. "If I have time."

"Oh I hope you do. I've got some money. I mean I
didn't expect you to work for free. But I think you'll like
it. It's called the Playhouse. We all played there when we
were kids."

"Marcella!" Ivy appeared on the other side of the desk,
emerging with the crowd from the auditorium.

"I was just showing Ms. Waterhouse how to get to her
room."

Salome picked up the map and said loudly for Ivy's
benefit, "Thanks for your help, Marcella. See you tomorrow."

THE STORM HAD NOT LET UP ONE BIT, IN
fact, it seemed to have increased in intensity. The wind
drove the rain horizontally, forcing Salome to bend nearly
double as she fought her way toward Watts House, her
bags gripped at her middle. Even though tucked into her
coat, her hair was pulled by the wind and whipped around
her head. The icy rain felt like shards of glass scouring
her forehead.

The house itself was at a diagonal from the main building, the last in the row of three and quite a pace from the
administration building. As she slowly plodded forward,
the sounds from the sea grew louder. She hoped the
booming surf wouldn't keep her awake all night. Even in
the calmer waters of Monterey Bay, there were nights
when she felt she was right in the water being battered
against the cliff.

Tightening her grip on the bags, she concentrated on
simply making it to Watts House before the wind picked
her up and spun her off into the night.

Chapter 5

JUST discernible on the brass plaque beside the door was the inscription:

Saints need sinners.
                              —*Alan Watts*

Salome entered the house and stood in the foyer, half dazed, taking a moment to catch her breath. Protected by the Drizabone, only the hem of her uniform suffered; soaking wet, the wool and silk blend was badly misshapen from having been stepped on during the trek from the administration building. It would be days before her shoes dried out, but she'd packed extra footwear along with additional uniforms—one a duplicate of the robe, the other consisting of formfitting black pants; a black, long-sleeved cashmere shirt; and a quilted black jacket with ceramic black and white tai chi discs for buttons.

Directly ahead, a fire crackled. On either side of the fireplace, dingy lace curtains fluttered lightly, indicating drafty windows. Sofas and snug overstuffed chairs were scattered around the room. Bookcases covered most of the wall space. The fire and furnishings gave the common room a homey, lived-in feel. In fair weather, the effect might be more along the lines of "tired and worn," but on such a cold, ragged night, no such criticisms were likely to be voiced.

Salome smelled coffee. Following her nose, she shuffled forward, careful to avoid tripping on the sloppy hem. In an alcove, a coffeepot steamed. There was also a table, some cupboards, a small refrigerator, and a pay phone on the wall. The latter told her the rooms didn't have phone service. No problem, she had her cell phone; if that failed, she had change.

Further on, two corridors branched off to the right and left.

"Wet enough for you?" A man, who'd been hidden in a high-backed armchair facing the fireplace, peeked around the side. He smiled broadly, lifting cheeks the size and color of red apples.

"Hi," Salome said.

"Two things. Don't expect to watch your favorite Friday night TV programs. No TV. Hmm, I bet you're a *Buffy the Vampire Slayer* fan."

Salome thought she must look rather witchy. "Frankly, I'm just anxious to get to my room." Before she could ask directions, he continued, leading her to think he might me a proctor.

"Second, no alcohol. But I've got a flask. You look like you could use a hot toddy."

"Anyone else here?" If he was the only one around, she might be wise to just find her room herself. Still, the house wasn't that big, and locating her room wouldn't be that much of a problem for her—or him.

"A few people have staggered in. Some holed up soon as they arrived—like me. You just get here, or did you go to the presentation?"

"Look, maybe we can chat later. I need to find my room."

"What am I thinking?" he said and got up from the chair. "Here, let me help you."

"Really. I can manage." She held her bags more tightly.

"What's your name?"

"Salome."

"Wow! Like the dancer. You bring your seven veils?"

Salome started to move off down the first corridor.

"We have something in common. I was named after a famous person, too. I'm Alan. Alan Watts."

That stopped her. "Really?"

"Really." He laughed. "My parents used to come here in the seventies. They said I was conceived in this very house. Couldn't resist coming down for the reopening. Rooms here are the most expensive, but I guess you know that. Kind of surprising."

"Why do you say that?"

"Wait'll you see your room. We're not talking five star accommodations. I'd heard the whole place had been remodeled back in the mid-nineties, when it was a retreat for rich techies. There was an article about it in the *Chronicle*. I think all they did though was fill the place with computers and hi-tech toys. Of course, they did spend some bucks on the administration building—"

"It's been nice talking to you, Alan, but I'm going to call it a night."

"Sure you don't want any help?"

"Quite sure. But thanks."

Salome moved off down the left corridor, the low numbers indicating she was in the correct wing. After a moment, she unlocked the door to number four, certainly not the number she would have chosen. According to Chinese numerology, the number four, because it sounded similar to the Cantonese word for "death," was unlucky—good enough reason to remember it.

As she pushed the door open, Alan appeared. She hoped she wouldn't have to do something rude—like deliver an elbow to his chest. He carried a cup of coffee.

"Thought you'd like some hot coffee," he said.

She felt a twinge of guilt but not enough to lower her guard.

"That's very thoughtful, Alan. Just put it on the floor."

"Hope you weren't expecting to connect with the Internet either. All the computers are gone. I didn't bring my laptop, figuring there'd be plenty here. But when I checked in, they said all the equipment had been sold. So the new Star Institute is computer-free."

A commotion and voices indicated new arrivals. Salome felt a little more secure.

"Have a good night," Alan said and went off down the corridor to be helpful. "Don't forget the coffee."

"Good night, Alan."

Before entering a residence for a consultation and before entering a hotel or motel room for the first time, Salome normally took a moment to clear her mind by chanting *om ma ni pad mi om* nine times, her hands in the proper mudra—left over right, thumbs nearly touching. Thus prepared, and with eyes closed, her first impression would not be clouded, enabling her to "read" the energies therein.

At the moment, her thoughts were so scattered it would take some time to reign them in. And there were the further distractions of noisy people and her own cold, numb feet and lower legs. She switched on the overhead light and dropped her bags on the thick orange shag carpeting, retrieved the mug of coffee, and locked the door. With her hands wrapped around the mug for warmth, she examined her accommodations, automatically superimposing the Bagua on the small room.

Straight ahead, in the wealth gua, was a single bed, the head under the window. The foot faced the door, the worst position for a bed in feng shui, as it was considered symbolic of death, a corpse being carried from a house feet first. Complicating the bad position was a full mirror on the back of the door. Mirrors should never face the bed. To wake in the night and be startled by one's ghostly image would damage body ch'i. As Phyllis had pointed out earlier, over time, this can lead to serious physical and mental problems. Nor should beds be directly under a window; energy coming from the window can adversely affect sleep.

She could predict the area of bodily discomfort, too. After a night in this bed, in the wealth gua, her bones and/ or hips would probably ache. Factoring in her age and definitely the cold damp weather, and that bones and hips were the body parts assigned to the wealth gua, she needed to implement some feng shui enhancements so she wouldn't wake up in pain.

An auspicious color, orange contained the power of red—to stimulate and negate the harmful effects of bad ch'i—and yellow's characteristic tolerance and wisdom. A good color for use in a living room, orange she considered too stimulating for the bedroom. Still, the color of the rug would counteract some of the negative aspects of the bed's placement.

Instead of a nightstand, a small desk and chair were beside the bed in the fame gua. On the opposite wall, in children/creativity, was a long, low dresser. A standard motel-type painting of a bland landscape, one that would neither stimulate creativity nor offend general sensibilities, hung above it. Instead of a closet there was a tubular metal shelf with a blanket on top and a bench below.

To the right of the door was the bathroom. She lowered the toilet seat and lid and peeked in the fiberglass, no-skid shower stall. A distorted mirror hung above the sink. At least everything was clean.

In just a couple minutes, she had assessed the room. A shower and unpacking would have to wait. She stripped to her long underwear and took her feng shui travel kit out of the carryall.

First she covered the mirror affixed to the door with a length of silk in soothing sea green. She moved the desk chair to the foot of the bed and screwed a hook into the ceiling. From it she hung a 30-mm faceted crystal on an eighteen-inch red cord. The crystal would disperse negative energy. She unwrapped a round glass containing a green, pine-scented candle, lit it, and placed it on the desk.

Using an atomizer, she sprayed the room and bath with a mixture of pure water and lavender oil. Both the candle and spray would get rid of the stagnant energy.

Finally, she rang a small brass bell nine times to chase out any sha, the dangerous, negative opposite of good ch'i, that settled in dark, dank, long-neglected spaces.

Feeling better now that the room had been taken care of, she pulled on her coat and went to her car for her hanging bag.

Once back in the room, she showered and changed into night wear.

WITH THE SOUND OF RAIN PELTING THE WINdow, Salome made herself comfortable on the bed, sitting Indian-style, a pillow at her back and against the wall. She wore a pink fleece sleep suit decorated with bunnies and sheepskin slippers, the fleecy interior keeping her feet toasty. The coffee was on the windowsill, reheated by a portable electric coil she'd brought from home. It did nothing for the taste, but at least the beverage was hot. Beside her were a notebook and pen and Phyl's folder containing information about Toby Ashcroft's murder. At some point she'd review the workshop plan, but that could wait for now.

She reached for the folder, then suddenly stopped and sat straighter. It wasn't exactly fear she felt, more a sense of being at the receiving end of seriously negative energy, or sha. A common form of sha came from the sharp edges of structures, which shot what were called poison arrows at anything in their path. To diffuse this potentially lethal energy, Salome recommended hanging a wooden Bagua with a mirror in the center outside and above the front door to deflect the arrows. In Hong Kong there had actually been "sha wars"—high-rise office buildings constructed with sharp edges aimed at their competitors. To retaliate, another high-rise would be mirrored, thus sending the poison arrows right back to the source.

Salome wondered what the source of her sudden unease could be. Was it something in a nearby room or coming from outside Watts House? She remembered seeing what might have been a sharp corner on the administration building when she first arrived, but the heavy rain had distorted the actual shape, and she'd been running at the time.

Her thoughts turned from feng shui possibilities to an actual human source, someone with extremely powerful negative energy. Immediately, Duncan Mah reappeared in her mind. Concern now turned to real fear. Despite her certainty now that Ross Prenderville had been the enraged driver, she still couldn't shake the idea of Mah's proximity.

She shut off the light and blew out the candle. Moving the curtain to one side, she peered out the window. The wind had diminished in strength, and the rain now fell at a less severe angle but was still as heavy as it had been when she was out in it. As her eyes adjusted, she could see the eucalyptus trees, their branches performing an erratic dance. You'd have to be a complete fool to be hanging out in this weather. Of all the things Duncan Mah may have been, a fool was not one of them. Then she realized how close Watts House was to the drive. It also appeared to be the closest structure to the pumpkin patch—where Toby Ashcroft had been murdered. The energy released by murder was extremely powerful and tenacious, permeating everything in its vicinity. Sensitive people picked up on it easily and often became terrified if they didn't know their own capacity for such things and if they didn't know about the violence that had taken place. Her room being the last on this side of the house, energy coming from the direction of the patch would hit her first.

She sat down on the edge of the bed. She could spend all night cataloging variables. However, there was one person who might be able to alleviate her fears about Duncan Mah.

After switching the lamp back on and relighting the candle, she picked up the cell phone and called a number in Washington, D.C. Judah Freeman kept strange hours, so calling at 1 A.M. Eastern Time wouldn't necessarily harm their decades-old friendship. If he wasn't available, it would do her good just to hear his comforting baritone ask her to leave a message.

"Freeman Agency."

"Jude! It's Salome. Did I wake you?"

His laugh boomed three thousand miles into her ear. She instantly pictured the former Washington, D.C., Metropolitan homicide detective leaning back in the swivel chair behind the massive desk suitable for his size. He was a big, sturdy, middle-aged African American, with gray patches branching out from the sides of his head. "I'm like Pinkerton's, Mei, I never sleep. What's up?"

Now that she had him on the phone, she felt silly.

"Oh, I don't know, Jude. It's just a weird night. Sorry I bothered you."

"Hey! You're not bothering me. What's bothering you?"

She took a breath. "I thought I saw Duncan Mah tonight."

Judah's voice lost its lightness. "Speak to me, kiddo."

After just a brief hesitation, she poured out the evening's relevant events, beginning with the incident on Highway 1 and concluding with identifying Ross Prenderville as the demon behind the wheel.

"You sure this Prenderville character isn't Mah?"

Salome jerked up and shivered. "God, Jude, now *you're* scaring me."

"Until he's caught or killed, you're going to have to deal with it. He's a phantom and a chameleon. By now he's probably got blonde hair, blue eyes, and is passing himself off as Grace Kelly's love child with Chairman Mao."

"Now that's creative morphing."

"As the bard of detectives said, 'Once you've eliminated the impossible, what remains, however improbable, must be the truth.' "

"Have you picked up anything at all in the past couple weeks?"

"Well, it is funny you calling now."

She felt as if someone had dropped ice down her back. Jude must have heard something about Duncan Mah.

Chapter 6

"YOU still there?" Jude asked.

Salome took a deep breath. "Yeah."

"The bad news or the good news first?"

"If he's alive, it's all bad."

"Hmm. Good point. Anyway," he sighed, "he might be on the west coast."

"Good grief, Jude. Where?"

At that moment, the light flickered. Vaguely, Salome wondered if the bulb needed to be replaced.

"Several robberies in Vancouver, British Columbia, seem to have his signature on them. All rich women lately involved with an attractive man of Chinese descent; all robbed in the past month."

Salome groaned.

"Thing is, and this is the good news, it's unlikely he'll be returning to the States anytime soon. It's still too hot for him here."

"I'll try to keep that in mind."

They chatted about generalities for a few minutes more then said good night.

Feeling somewhat reassured, she took a couple deep breaths and settled in. Then, just as she opened the file on her lap, the light went out. The green candle on the desk provided light, so she wasn't in complete darkness.

Thinking the bulb had burned out, she used the edge of the sheet to protect her hand and unscrewed it. Draping the Drizabone over her shoulders, she started for the door, hoping replacement bulbs were in the pantry where she'd seen the coffee maker. Then she heard a commotion in the hall and groaned inwardly. Now thinking there might have been a blackout, she opened the door, and her suspicion was confirmed.

The hall was in darkness, as were the rooms revealed by open doors. Beyond, she could see the glow cast by the fire in the common room. People were moving about, those in robes reminiscent of monks at a retreat—a barebones retreat without electricity.

Salome turned around and picked up her empty coffee cup. Hopefully there would be a hot beverage still available. The heat was powered by electricity—or rather, no longer powered by electricity.

There was enough indirect light from the fireplace for her to make her way to the pantry by the front door. She stood to one side, as several people came out, steam just visible trailing from their cups. By the time she entered, the coffeepot was empty, but the hot water pot was half full. So there would be more to go around, she allowed herself only half a cup.

"Damn! No coffee!" a woman said, shaking the pot.

"There's still some hot water," Salome said and stepped into the foyer. She'd brought tea in her carryall along with emergency rations and didn't have to fumble in the dark pantry looking for tea bags.

"People! People!" A figure stood silhouetted against the fireplace. She recognized Alan Watts's voice. "I've just talked to someone in the administration building. It appears we have a blackout. Not just us, the entire area."

Someone nearby said, "Why do these things always happen on weekends?"

Alan went on, "I suggest everyone just go to bed. Got

a good supply of firewood, so we're in luck there. And, we're the only house with a fireplace, so if word gets out, we may have company. Most people are probably asleep already. But if you hear activity, don't worry, just go back to sleep, it'll probably be the insomniacs coming over for a warm-up."

"Tolkien House has a fireplace. They're on the other side of the administration building," someone called out.

"They've probably got the Ring Wraiths and Orcs, too," Alan said.

The laughter dissipated some of the tension. Salome decided that Alan was a good guy to have around in a crisis.

"If there're no objections, I've appointed myself as house monitor and will be here if you need anything. PG&E has been alerted, and crews are already working to restore the electricity. Like I said, the whole area is affected; lots of people besides us."

"What about candles?"

"Haven't had time to look, but there might be some in the pantry. If not, I'll check with administration."

Salome returned to her room and added a bag of green tea to her rapidly cooling water. She had another candle in her carryall but decided not to donate it unless someone came asking.

Too wide-awake now to fall asleep, she made a nest of the covers and the extra blanket and began to read. The candlelight softly illuminating Phyllis's typed notes increased the eerie nature of Toby Ashcroft's death.

Using his cell phone, John Gray, the man who, along with his three children, had found the body of Tobias Ashcroft, called the police at 4:26 P.M. on October 30. The police had arrived within twenty minutes of the call. Because his frightened children were crying, Gray was quickly questioned and released.

The victim's throat had been cut, and he'd bled to death. The medical examiner determined time of death to be around midnight on October 29, give or take an hour or two. So, by the time his body was found, he'd been dead a good sixteen to eighteen hours. Stomach contents revealed that he'd consumed chocolate cream-filled cakes, cream-filled sponge cakes, corn chips, salsa, and soft drinks about an hour before death. His body was clean, and soap residue was found in the toe- and fingernail clippings, along with traces of salt, corn matter, chocolate, and sponge cake.

Other than ants that had invaded the wound, the body showed no signs of animal interference. Blood had soaked the burlap mask along the line of the wound, some penetrating the narrow length of clothesline that had been used to keep the mask in place. Blood had also soaked into the ground beneath his head, but considering that he'd bled to death, the amount appeared to be a few pints low.

Most likely the murder weapon was the knife he used to carve the jack-o'-lanterns. The type of blade, as described by Marcella Cruz, seemed to match the cut across the neck.

When first interviewed by detectives at 5:30 P.M. on October 30, Marcella Cruz said she'd last seen Toby the day before when she took him lunch at two. Lunch consisted of a big bowl of chili in an insulated carrier, sticks of celery, and a bag of tortilla chips. He had taken the food and wandered across the road to the cliffs. He commonly ate his lunch on the cliff where he could watch the sea. Marcella then drove to Santa Cruz to stay the night with a girlfriend. She spent the next day running various errands in Santa Cruz and returned about four. She was fixing stew when the homicide detectives appeared at her door.

Marcella did odd jobs around Ashcroft Farms and lately had been enlisted to help prepare the institute for its reopening, doing everything from cleaning the different houses to secretarial work. She lived in a cottage known as the Playhouse that sat at the top of the hill, a five-minute walk from the pumpkin patch. After the autopsy, she was questioned again. No, Marcella did not believe that Toby had come up to the Playhouse on the 29th to take a shower—she would have seen evidence in the bathroom. Not a very tidy person, at the very least, Toby would have left a wet towel on the floor. Besides, he lived in the Big House across the road and in the middle of the hill. If he wanted to take a shower, he'd use his own bathroom.

Marcella, of Ohlone and Hispanic descent, had known Toby since childhood. Her father had been manager of Ashcroft Farms dairy and had been given a small house. She and Toby were the same age and had been good friends all their lives. She'd moved to Oregon after high school, when Toby went on to Stanford. Marcella returned two years ago, at which time she'd resumed employment with the Ashcrofts and Toby had given her the use of the Playhouse. And no, she no longer used drugs or alcohol and had been clean and sober since returning to California.

Ivy Ashcroft had been shopping in San Francisco on October 29. She met Ross Prenderville, and they went to dinner and a movie, then she drove him to his house in Davenport and returned home about 11 P.M. Toby's rooms were on the first floor, and the doors were closed. She did not hear anything and went directly upstairs to her rooms, took a shower, and went to bed.

The next morning Ivy revisited San Francisco to continue shopping for various things they needed for the upcoming opening of the institute. She didn't return until about 6 P.M., which is when she had learned about her brother's murder. She decided not to cancel the weekend of workshops because to do so would not be in anyone's best interests. She and Toby had wanted the institute to be a going concern, and by the number of people they'd had to turn down, being able to accommodate only about seventy-five, she felt certain it would be a success and necessary source of revenue.

In Ivy's statement, she mentioned Toby and Marcella's

relationship. She thought that Marcella was still doing drugs, although her brother had insisted she was clean and sober. They seemed close, as they had been as children, but Ivy believed that Toby would never consider Marcella as a love interest. Quite simply, Marcella was not his social or intellectual equal.

Ivy said that she and Ross Prenderville were engaged to be married, but the date was not yet set. She'd met Prenderville through Toby and Toys for Techies. Prenderville had been one of the early partners and the dot com's attorney. Before devoting her time to reopening the institute, Ivy had been in the marketing department of a famous brand-name clothing store, the head office in San Francisco. She had an M.B.A. from Stanford, matriculating two years before her brother received his undergraduate degree there in computer science. Instead of going to graduate school, Toby had gone to work for IBM in Silicon Valley and after several years started his own dot com, Toys for Techies.

During the heady days of the dot com's success, Toby had turned the institute into a retreat for wealthy dot-comers like himself. Ivy told the police that Toby had gotten so into playing and having a good time, he had let his business flounder. He neglected to collect payment from those who continued to use the institute and was taken advantage of. By the time he got around to sending the bills, the people who owed him were losing their own businesses. He did manage to pay off what he owed and avoided bankruptcy.

Ross Prenderville backed up Ivy's statement about meeting for dinner on the night of the 29th and his being driven home that evening. A neighbor, who let the cat out every night before the 10 o'clock news, said she had seen Ross exit Ivy's car and enter his house. Ross had spent the following day working at home and learned of the murder when Ivy telephoned him.

The workers at the dairy rarely took notice of activity

on the other side of the hill. The dairy itself was about a quarter mile inland east of the Big House.

Since both their parents were dead, Ivy and Toby held joint ownership of the estate, which included the dairy, institute, and pumpkin farm. Toby's and Ivy's wills were nearly identical. Toby had left everything to Ivy, unless he had progeny at the time of his death, in which case, his portion of the estate would go to the child or children and the mother. Ivy's beneficiary was Toby, unless she was married at the time of her death, in which case, her portion of the estate would go to her husband, and if she had any, her children.

A search of the grounds and all buildings had revealed nothing, no murder weapon, and no drugs, nothing that would point the finger at anyone.

Toby's former business partners were questioned but all had tight alibis, though some had strong motives—the loss of millions didn't inspire gratitude.

On the morning of the 31st, John Gray gave a formal statement to the police. Gray, a graduate student at a local university, claimed to have last seen Toby alive October 29th, when he stopped to purchase a jack-o'-lantern and had returned on the 30th, because his wife wanted several more. He had never met or seen Toby Ashcroft before the 29th. Yes, he knew of Ashcroft Farms dairy and that the pumpkin patch was part of the operation but thought Toby was just a farm laborer. And no, he'd never invested in Toys for Techies.

Besides the missing murder weapon, the money box, which Marcella said usually contained fifty dollars in coins and low-denomination bills plus whatever money he made each day, was gone. It was possible Toby had been murdered for the cash. He could have been lured from the stand on the pretext of, say, going for a beer with someone he knew, perhaps someone he had met recently. That person might then have killed him at another location and returned his body the next morning.

* * *

SALOME SLIPPED THE FOLDER BACK IN HER satchel. The temperature in the room had dropped considerably. She rubbed her cold, numbing hands together then got up. She set the flashlight on the desk within easy reach, put a change of clothes—jeans, T-shirt, cable knit sweater, socks and boots—on the desk chair, draping the Drizabone over the back, propping the umbrella against one of the legs. In spite of the feng shui applications, the energy in the room still felt strange and far from harmonious. Had she been the sort to carry a weapon, she would have put it under her pillow. Should anything else occur in the night, she wanted to be prepared. Tomorrow she'd make a thorough search of the area to find the source of the sha, or bad energy.

Feeling somewhat secure, she blew out the candle and curled up under the covers. The effects of the long day, which had begun on an early morning flight from San Diego, managed to scuttle the cacophony outside—the gunshot crackle of waves just before breaking, the crash as they hit the beach, the rain's aggressive, unrelenting strikes against the house, the trees battering each other in the high wind. Finally, she dozed off.

Chapter 7

SALOME shot up in bed, her heart racing. She was late for her lecture. People had been waiting for hours while she trudged through knee-deep mud to get to the classroom. She carried a Bagua made of concrete. With each painfully slow step, the classroom moved farther away.

She blinked. The room gradually came into focus, but just enough to let her know she'd been dreaming. Then she realized the storm had abated somewhat and wondered if the quiet had awakened her. But there wasn't quiet, not *in* the house. Outside the door to her room, a commotion was going on. She could hear voices raised in anger, doors banging, and general activity. She pulled on her Driza-bone, grabbed the flashlight, and looked at her watch. It was just after 4 A.M. She went to investigate.

The common room still glowed with firelight, and as she approached, she saw shadowy figures coming into the house, heard the door bang. After just a moment, the smell hit her. A couple other people in the hall gasped and put their hands over their noses and mouths.

"What the hell—"

Then she heard Alan. "People, people! *Please!* Leave

your shoes outside! We'll try to accommodate you but please lose the shoes!"

Salome came upon a couple huddled beside the hallway. They were probably in their mid-seventies. The man had his arm around the woman. She was only about five feet two, he maybe two inches taller. Her expression was one of fear and hostility as she jumped from one bare foot to the other. He was trying to soothe her. They wore down jackets over robes and pajamas.

"What's going on?" Salome asked.

"The toilets overflowed in Ram Dass House," the man said. "The house is flooded with raw sewage."

"My feet are like ice cubes!" the woman snapped, jumping from one foot to the other.

"We took our slippers off soon as we got outside. A lot of other people didn't do that, and they're tracking shit in here."

Salome looked around for a moment. People were crowding onto the sofas and chairs, a few sitting resignedly on the floor. "There's much more room in the administration building," she said.

"Yeah, but it's freezing over there. Floors are granite."

Someone dashed by, jostling the couple.

"Look, why don't you come to my room?" Salome asked.

The woman twisted her wedding rings around so the diamonds were inside her palm. Not a trusting soul.

"Let's just get out of the way," Salome said. With her hand on the man's arm, she pulled the couple into the hall, leading the way with her flashlight.

"We're in the Elder Hostel program," the man said. "I'm Stephen Greenwald, and this is my wife, Delores."

"I'm Salome Waterhouse."

"Our last trip was to Mexico, to study Mayan astrology," Stephen started.

Delores piped in. "Our accommodations were much nicer! In Mexico!"

"No one controls the weather, honey bun. This is just a fluke."

"My behind! Old plumbing's the reason. They just didn't want to spend money."

"The plumbing in my room is just fine. In fact, you can have the room, but I'm afraid the bed's a single."

"We'll manage," Delores said.

"But where will you stay?" Stephen asked, as Salome opened the door.

"I can stay quite comfortably in my car."

"That doesn't sound good," Stephen replied, genuine concern on his face.

"She's young, Stephen. And limber."

Stephen and Delores hovered by the door, as Salome went in and lit the candle, half smiling to herself. Age, after all, was relative.

Delores moved into the bathroom. "I'll just wash my feet."

Stephen hesitated in the doorway.

"Don't worry about me, Mr. Greenwald. Come on in. I'll be fine."

"I'd feel better if I knew everyone was out of Ram Dass."

"Not your problem, Stephen," Delores called out from the bathroom. "If they can sleep through the stink, more power to them."

"Disease, honey bun."

"I won't have you stumbling around in the dark," Delores retorted and poked her head out of the bathroom. "Would you shine that light in here, honey. Can't see a damn thing."

"I'm going back," Stephen said. "May I borrow your flashlight? Won't take five minutes."

Salome was glad to accommodate these people, but she wouldn't part with her light. Not that she didn't trust him; any number of things might happen and she needed it to get to her car in good order, without stumbling around in the dark herself. "I'll go with you."

Salome slipped on her boots, snapped the two panels of her Drizabone shut, and grabbed the umbrella.

Delores blocked the door. "Someone might think you're looting!"

Stephen held her shoulders firmly, gave her a peck on the cheek, and moved her to the side.

"Make yourself comfortable, Delores. We'll be back in a few minutes."

Outside, Stephen huddled beside Salome under the umbrella. "Don't even need the light. Just follow our noses," he said.

Wind and rain had diminished in intensity as the tail end of the latest squall headed inland. In just a moment they reached Ram Dass House. It was a simple clapboard structure with half a dozen small windows on either side of the main door. Salome shone the light. Water jeweled a polished brass plate beside the door. It read:

BE HERE NOW
—Ram Dass

Stephen nodded at the message. "Looks like we are." He stepped to the side of the door politely. "The rooms are tiny—Delores called them cells. So it shouldn't take but a minute or two to make sure everyone's out. And if we wake someone, so be it. At least they'll know what's happened. If they want to stay, that's up to them."

The stench was terrible. The light reflected off the wet surface of the floor. Straight ahead were the communal bathrooms, women's facilities on the left, men's on the right. Both doors were propped open.

The front door opening on a bathroom was one of the worst configurations in feng shui and represented all sorts of problems, certainly unsound finances. Salome could understand the house being built with simplicity in mind, but a bathroom should not be the first thing seen upon entering a building. She felt strongly that the house's history included many small catastrophes.

"Hello!" Stephen called out. They moved first down the corridor to the left then down the corridor on the right. Most doors were closed, a few stood open. At the locked doors, Salome knocked, while Stephen repeated, "Hello, anybody in there?"

"The cheap seats," Stephen said, referring to the stark cubicles furnished with narrow cots, a tiny table and gooseneck lamp, and a stand for a piece of luggage.

Halfway down the right corridor, Salome said, "Why didn't you just leave by the window? Would have saved trooping through the muck."

"Couldn't get the damn thing open. The frame must have swelled in all this rain. To make it worse, there's about a hundred coats of paint. Not bothering to strip the old paint before applying the new tells me something about the management. I can forgive toilets backing up, but not taking care of simple safety measures is inexcusable."

They encountered no one. Salome started back toward Watts House, intending to collect her things and move into the truck. The passenger seat folded down, and she could stretch out—

She'd gone about five feet, when Stephen stopped her. "Wait a minute. We haven't checked the windows."

"If anyone was in there, they'd have heard us."

"You go on, then. There were a couple elderly ladies . . . I just want to make sure they didn't try to get out a window and have a heart attack or something."

Salome turned around. She held the umbrella and shined the light, while he checked each window. The effort seemed futile, since curtains prevented a view of each room.

They were halfway down the backside of the house, finishing the inspection, when they came to a window partially open. Stephen poked his head inside. Suddenly quite agitated, he extended his arm, snapping his fingers. "Give me that flashlight."

Then he crawled inside.

"Stephen, what are you doing?"

But Stephen didn't answer, until, a long minute later she heard, "Holy Cow!"

The two nearly butted heads, as Salome started to have a look inside and Stephen suddenly tried to get out. Salome pulled her head back just in time. He seemed to be having trouble getting out. She grabbed the flashlight then took his arm and felt his body shaking violently.

"Take it easy, Mr. Greenwald," she said in a calm voice, fearing he might have a seizure.

"Get an ambulance!" he croaked breathlessly.

She helped him to the ground. "What did you see?"

He swallowed hard. "Looks like she slipped and fell."

"One of the elderly women?"

He shook his head then wiped the rain from his face. "No. It's someone else. Dark hair. Short. She's lying face-down on the floor. Not moving. I couldn't find a pulse. Maybe you should check."

Salome shone the light and peered in through the window. Head toward the door, the body appeared rigid and wore a pink chenille robe, which was, but for the back, soaked in effluvia. From Salome's vantage point, it appeared that the woman's feet were also free of muck. Her hair wasn't short, but rather pulled tightly into the distinctive style of French braids, the lengths of which had fallen forward and were under her torso. Beyond the obvious, something wasn't right.

"Either go in or let's get to a phone!" Stephen blurted.

She didn't want to alarm him further by mentioning the word "crime scene," but if that's what it was, she'd best not enter. Stephen had already disturbed the area but couldn't be faulted.

She pulled her head out. Stephen took off.

"Wait!"

Salome ran after him, her feet splashing in the standing water. "Stephen, stop! There are a lot of people around here. We don't want to cause a panic."

At the end of the house he halted, shivering more with fear, Salome thought, than cold. "Pay phone's just inside the door," he sputtered.

"I think we'd best go to the administration building. Someone's probably there waiting for the PG&E crew and to take care of any emergencies."

Stephen nodded vacantly.

They moved off toward the administration building, Salome keeping a firm grip on Stephen in case he stumbled. His body trembled. After a moment, he jerked his arm from her grasp, probably embarrassed that he'd momentarily lost his composure.

Ahead something rose up from the ground. Salome vaguely thought of the prow of a ship. As they came closer, she could see a sharp metallic edge looming so high the top was lost in the misty darkness.

"Good God, what the hell is that?"

"A point of the star," Stephen said.

Salome stopped, the beam of the flashlight weak against the enormous structure. She felt instant dread and for a moment, couldn't speak.

"Haven't you seen it? The building's shaped like a star. *Star Institute*. Get it?"

Without answering, she turned and looked toward Watts House, still hidden in the darkness behind the fog and rain. The point, *a poison arrow* aimed right in that direction.

Chapter 8

☯

"How many points are there?"

"Who cares!" Stephen Greenwald snapped. "Let's get this over with. Delores'll be worried."

At the central desk, Marcella shot up from her chair. Her face was shadowed in the light from several candles, but Salome could clearly read the apprehension that appeared the moment she and Greenwald rushed inside.

The instant he said "body in Ram Dass," Marcella grabbed the phone. Into the receiver she said, "Let me speak to Ivy." Then, "I don't care if she's asleep! This is an emergency!"

After a pause, she began calmly, but her aggravation grew. "There's a body in Ram Dass . . . no, I don't know who . . . not yet. I thought you should know first . . . all right, soon as I hang up . . . but this isn't my responsibility. You better get down here this time!"

Marcella disconnected the line and called 911, her breathing heavy.

"I'm going back to Delores," Stephen declared.

"Stephen, you'll have to talk to the authorities."

"Not before I check in with Delores."

He took the flashlight and disappeared into the rain, before Salome could hand over the umbrella.

Marcella put down the receiver and shook her head. She wore a heavy coat that had seen many winters; every one of them now seemed etched on her face.

"I think I just lost my job." She leaned forward and put her head on her arms.

"It'll be fine. People react to death in funny ways," Salome said and squeezed her arm. "Listen would you look up something for me?"

"Sure." Marcella rose and wiped a tear from her eye, forcing a smile. "Been a bad couple of weeks."

"There was a woman at my table tonight. Carla Whitmore. Where is she staying?"

"I'm not really supposed to give that information out," Marcella said, as she unlocked a drawer behind the desk, her manner offhand, like someone on the last day of a job. "But I'll bet you have a good reason for asking." She retrieved a folder. "Ram Dass. Room nine, north side of the house."

"Would that be next to the bathroom?"

"As you enter, in the right corridor."

Salome nodded. "Hmm. I admired her French braids. Never could get the hang of it. My hair and fingers get all twisted together."

"Guess I'll need keys," Marcella muttered and dropped a key ring in her pocket. She returned the folder and re-locked the drawer. "You think it's Carla?"

"Just because of the French braids. You know her?"

"Actually, I do. She's a social worker with Indian health services up in the city. Keeps track of people with drug and drinking problems. We're not friends or anything. She gave me a list of places to go for AA meetings when I moved back here a couple years ago. A nice woman but a little too much of a crusader, if you know what I mean."

"So she might have made a few enemies?" Salome tried

to sound casual. But a couple of things about the body now were clearer. That the back of the robe and the soles and heels of the feet were dry, led her to believe that Carla Whitmore was dead before the toilets flooded. If she had been alive at the time of the flooding and was leaving the room, why was the window open but her head facing the door? Having succeeded in opening the window—difficult as Stephen pointed out—why choose to exit through the door, which required that she walk through sewage?

". . . bureaucrats."

"Excuse me?"

"Bureaucrats. She wasn't popular with bureaucrats. She was always after more money for Indian health programs."

"Married? Divorced?"

"Afraid I don't know anything about her personal life."

"Was she Indian?"

Marcella shrugged and moved out from behind the desk. "Don't really know. It's hard to tell anymore unless you're living on the rez. Blood's so diluted. My family's Ohlone and Hispanic."

The two women approached the glass doors.

"A lot of us Indians work at the dairy. My father was manager for years until he retired."

"The Ashcroft dairy?"

"Only one around here. Just over the hill. Where I grew up."

"So you've known Ivy and, uh, her brother all your life?"

"Best friends when we were little."

"In that case, I'm sure you still have a job."

Marcella stiffened, her face suddenly wiped of all expression. "They're here," she said. In the distance, they could just make out the multicolored lights of EMS and police vehicles turning into the drive. "At least they're smart enough not to use the sirens. This place would be a zoo!"

She pushed open the door just as Stephen Greenwald emerged from the heavy mist, a bath towel on his head.

"Got my shoes," he said breathlessly. "Thank God Delores was asleep."

"Better flag them down before they tear up the grass," Marcella cried and dashed out, headed for the drive.

"Come on, Stephen," Salome urged and took his arm. They moved at a brisk pace toward Ram Dass House. "Did you talk to anyone?" she asked.

"Of course not! Anyway, bunch of people were huddled around the fire telling ghost stories. Won't be long before they've got a real one to talk about."

Salome led Stephen to the front door of Ram Dass House. If there had been foul play and the killer entered through the window, Salome wanted to avoid further trampling the ground. Not that it mattered that much—good prints would be difficult to come by in the slushy, muddy ground. Still, she was a great respecter of crime scenes.

They'd just caught their breath when pairs of paramedics, uniformed cops, and firemen—the fire department always present on the scene of a sudden death—came around the side of the house led by Marcella. They all crowded just inside. Marcella pulled the keys from her pocket then gagged. With her hand over her mouth, she handed over the keys to the nearest police officer then dashed outside and vomited.

The cop unlocked the door to room number nine, allowing only one paramedic to enter, while he stood just outside the room. Preferring the rain to the stink inside the house, the others began to move outside. Curiosity kept Salome in place, straining to hear what was said in room nine above the constant patter of the rain and the banter of the cops and emergency services personnel.

After a moment, Salome heard the paramedic say something about bruising, then "petechiae," which she knew were tiny hemorrhages in the eyes and on the skin that accompanied strangulation. The cop ordered the paramedic out of the room then closed the door.

"Who found the body?" the policeman asked.

When he'd established the particulars of the body's discovery, he told Salome and Greenwald to go on back to the administration building with Marcella and wait. Someone would be along shortly to talk to them.

Marcella rushed on ahead. Salome and Stephen Greenwald cleaned their shoes in the wet grass before entering the cold administration building. Salome went into the bathroom where Marcella was splashing water on her face.

"Are you all right?" Salome asked.

"I'll be fine." Her ashen complexion belied the statement.

"How long have you been here?"

"Since the blackout. Ivy called and told me to stay at the desk in case people had questions."

"Maybe you should lie down. Better yet, get someone down here to relieve you."

Marcella dismissed the suggestion with a wave of her hand.

"Let me call Ivy. It's her responsibility to handle emergencies."

"She'll be here. Just takes her forever to get dressed."

"Surely there's a Coke machine around. A soda would settle your stomach."

"Vending machines went out with the computers. Even if there was one it wouldn't be working without electricity."

Salome put her arm around Marcella and helped her back into the rotunda.

"How about juice then? There must be juice in the kitchen."

Marcella perked a little. "Hey, yeah. Thanks for reminding me. I completely forgot." Taking a candle, she moved down the corridor, hunched over in her coat. Then she disappeared from view, taking the stairs down to the basement.

Deciding that Marcella would be all right, Salome checked on Stephen. He was curled on one of the wooden benches by the door, dozing. Salome picked up one of the candles and had a look around.

Walking down the south corridor off the central desk, she first came to the men's rest room then a small, sparsely furnished office and, following the curve, discovered three classrooms, each in the crotch of the exterior extending walls. In each was a floor-to-ceiling window, a blackboard, and three long tables with chairs for about fifteen to twenty people. Taped to the doors were sheets of paper, indicating the early workshops and the names of the instructors. She didn't find herself on the south side.

The north side was identical with the exception of stairs leading down to the kitchen. She found her name on the door of the classroom located in the family/health gua and rather liked that.

Carrying a grocery bag, Marcella was just climbing the stairs when Salome was heading back to the central desk, having finished her quick tour.

"Is the kitchen nice?" Salome asked. Whatever was located at the foundation of a structure would influence activity above. The space should always be clean and free of clutter.

"All electric, which means not so nice, I guess. I don't know what to do about breakfast. Without the dumbwaiters functioning, I'll have to carry everything up. Of course that means no cooking either."

Marcella placed two one-gallon jugs of apple juice and a stack of paper cups on the counter. "Help yourself, Ms. Waterhouse."

"Please, let's forget the formality. Call me Salome."

She smiled. In the candlelight, Salome could see that Marcella had regained some color.

"I'm gonna take one of these," she lifted one of the jugs, "to the guys. I'll be back in just a few minutes."

Watching Marcella melt into the darkness, Salome realized that it was this young woman who possessed the proprietary feelings for the institute, the sense of stewardship apparently lacking in Ivy. A crisis swiftly and mercilessly reveals the truth of a person's character. In a more perfect world, Marcella, not Ivy, would own the Star Institute.

A DISTINGUISHED-LOOKING MAN, WEARING boots and a crisp raincoat over casual clothes, breezed into the rotunda, followed by another plainclothes detective of less regal bearing and a uniformed cop.

"Hello, Marcella," he greeted, their familiarity with each other leading Salome to believe she was in the company of Phyl's love interest and the lead detective on the Ashcroft murder.

Marcella immediately introduced Mr. Greenwald as the person who found the body.

Despite the hour and all he'd been through, fatigue vanished from the elderly man's face. Terror apparently made him alert.

"Hello, Mr. Greenwald. I'm detective Child." He turned to Marcella. "Is there an office where we might have some privacy?"

"Oh, sure." Carrying a candle, she stood outside the office just off the rotunda on the south side.

"I don't know about you, Mr. Greenwald, but I think I'd rather talk someplace more sweet smelling. Looks like you could use a cup of hot coffee."

Stephen Greenwald grabbed Salome's arm. "This young lady was with me."

Salome confirmed the fact. "I'm Salome Waterhouse."

He regarded her for a long moment then turned to Marcella. "Any chance of rustling up some coffee?"

"As you can see, the electricity's still out."

"I just thought you might have some stashed away in a thermos. I need you to get me the layout of the grounds and each building.

"Mr. Greenwald you go ahead and have a seat in the office. I'll be right with you."

Salome put her hand over Mr. Greenwald's. "It's okay."

While Greenwald shuffled off, looking like he was headed for the Grand Inquisitor's chamber of horrors, Child turned to the plainclothes detective. "No one is to leave the grounds. Anyone enters the administration building, put them in the auditorium and tell them if they try to leave they'll be arrested. We'll need a squad car to block the parking lot. These New Agers are early risers, so I want a uniform stationed in each house to take statements—just the basics—as people get up. Send them over here. I want to talk to every one of them before they can leave. Keep the press out. Limit their space to just outside the grounds.

"Oh yeah, call and have someone bring coffee—lots of it."

"Right." The plainclothes detective moved over by the front door and began talking on his handheld radio. Mr. Greenwald stopped just outside the office.

Salome was beginning to think she'd imagined introducing herself when Child finally said, "Any relation to Phyllis Waterhouse?"

"We're cousins."

"I'll talk to you as soon as I finish with Mr. Greenwald."

He went over to Mr. Greenwald.

"Tell you one thing, Officer, you won't catch me and my wife back here, not in this lifetime! From now on we're sticking with Elder Hostel."

Chapter 9

"SO you're Phyllis's cousin," Detective Child said, once Salome was seated on the other side of an ordinary metal desk on which the candle flickered. Without the raw glare of electric light, Child appeared as menacing as the gloomy shadows filling every corner.

"Yes." She noticed writing on the notebook in front of him but couldn't make it out.

Detective Child regarded her for a long moment. Salome could see his mind working, determining what to say and what not to say. "Ah yes, the murder at the Perfume Mansion—your property, right?"

"Right." He and Phyllis must have discussed the case. And why not? Phyllis had headed the investigation. Did he know she had been a suspect?

Then he surprised her. "I very much enjoy your husband's books."

"My *ex* husband. Next time I have the chance, I'll tell him. He likes positive feedback, especially from cops— the police." Phyllis must have told him about her former marriage to best-selling mystery author Gabriel Hoya. Salome's proximity to a wealthy, famous writer would certainly merit mention.

"So, we've established that you're familiar with criminal investigations. You know not to leave anything out."

"I'll do my best."

He took a small tape recorder from his pocket, stated the particulars of the interview, then set the recorder between them. The tape spun soundlessly.

"You're a feng shui practitioner, right?"

"Right. You use the proper pronunciation," she said, pleased that he hadn't mangled the words as so often happened. *Fung shuway.*

"You might say I'm familiar with it," he said. He straightened himself and lifted his chin. "Tell me what happened tonight."

"First, is the victim Carla Whitmore?"

"You know her?"

She smiled to herself. Already she'd goofed. *He* would ask the questions.

"Never met her before tonight. She sat next to me at the presentation dinner."

"Did you talk?"

"Just briefly. After my presentation she, Carla Whitmore that is, suggested I direct my attention to victims of domestic violence."

"Why did she say that?"

"At the time I thought it was just an observation," Salome said, then told him about her conversation with Marcella after she and Stephen Greenwald had found the body. "Because she was a social worker, I imagine she had experience with domestic violence."

"Why were you talking about her to Marcella?"

"I thought Carla might be the victim—her distinctive hairstyle provided the clue. French braids."

"So tell me about Mr. Stephen Greenwald. How did you meet him, and why were you with him when he found the body?"

Salome quickly gave her version, knowing that just a few moments prior Stephen had related his. She hoped Stephen told the same story. If he had reason to lie, her life would become much more complicated. She took extra care with minor details, such as her intention to sleep in the car. She vaguely considered backing up and mentioning the call to Judah but vetoed that idea; no sense cluttering his plate with her personal concerns. Perhaps later, if they spoke again, she'd tell him about Duncan Mah. It was then that her encounter with Ross Prenderville came to mind, and she had no compunction to hold back.

"Since you reminded me that no detail is too obscure in a murder investigation, I think I should tell you about an incident that occurred a short time before I arrived at the institute."

When she'd finished, Detective Child sat forward in his chair and played with the pen on his notepad. "You say you recognized him in the red candlelight when he sat down after singing, because it was just like the red dashboard light."

"Yes." Did he think she was being imaginative?

"But you're not absolutely certain?"

Salome sighed. "I'm absolutely certain he was driving a gold Lexus."

"But you didn't get the plate number?"

"When he moved ahead of me, I was heading for a tree on the side of the road. Check with the DMV," Salome said, lack of sleep beginning to make her impatient and nervy.

But he didn't seem to take offense, didn't remind her that he knew his job.

The door opened, and a young officer carrying a large white bag entered. He placed two lidded Styrofoam cups on the desk then added a handful of cream containers, sugar packets, and two red stirrers.

"Thanks, Morse. Next time, knock first."

"Oh! Sorry, sir."

When the officer left, Child popped the lids and actually reached across the desk to hand her a cup. "It just occurred to me that maybe coffee isn't the beverage of choice for feng shui practitioners."

"If it's hot and loaded with caffeine, I'll drink it." She turned down the offer of cream and sugar. He loaded his cup with both.

"Ever drink maté?"

"Sure. It's a good mental stimulant."

"You think it helps your work?"

Salome shrugged, wondering what he was leading up to. She didn't have long to wait.

"The wife of a good friend of mine hired a practitioner from San Francisco. As part of the program, he told her to throw away nine things each day for nine days."

Salome took a breath, sensing a new tension in the room.

"That sound familiar?"

"It's a way to start being aware of clutter and what you have as opposed to what you really need."

"Must be what she was thinking, when she moved my friend out and moved the practitioner in." He sat back and sipped his coffee. "It amazes me what people like you get away with. Just waltz right in to someone's house—move this, toss that, hang a mirror, and by the way, that husband of yours takes up too much room, so while you're at it, get rid of him, too."

She'd heard it all before. "There is a great deal of trust involved and a great deal of responsibility on the part of the practitioner."

There was a loud knock on the door.

"Come in!"

Salome turned her head to see Officer Morse poke his head in the door and bark excitedly, "Blood's been found in the chapel, sir. It's all over these blue—"

"Thank you, Morse," Child interrupted. "That'll be all!"

Child swept the notebook, pen, and tape recorder into his pockets and abruptly stood.

"We're not finished yet, but maybe you'd like to change

out of that bunny suit." He moved around the desk and opened the door. "Marcella?"

Salome joined him at the door. Marcella stood outside.

"Ms. Waterhouse needs to change clothes. Would you escort her to her room? Be back in ten minutes."

"I need time to clean up, too."

"Make it fifteen minutes."

Why Marcella, she wondered, and not a police escort? Maybe he did trust in the powers of a feng shui practitioner, figuring Marcella would open up and freely divulge some secret. Or maybe he thought Marcella could extract some tidbit out of her. Well, he'd created too much negative static for her to allow him to use her. Unless Marcella confessed to killing Carla Whitmore—or Toby Ashcroft—Salome would not repeat anything they might discuss.

Salome nodded and swept out of the office, trying to regain some dignity, anger adding a spring to her steps. Once outside, she raised her arms and flicked the middle fingers of both hands against her thumbs to throw off the negative energy.

Marcella looked amused. "Does it work?"

"Try it."

Marcella did. "Wow! Cool."

The night's violent labor had birthed an exquisite morning. For a moment, the two women stood quietly, in awe of their surroundings. The sky was a dome of blue crystal streaked with pink and violet. The grass was brilliant emerald, studded with dewy rainbows. But out to sea, dense gray clouds heralded the approach of another Pacific storm system.

"This is what it's all about—or should be," Marcella said softly. "Not tantric sex or self-love or anything can do a body as much good as being in the middle of a beautiful place. Look at those colors. And the ocean. Calm as a lake."

Salome glanced at the houses to her right: Watts, Leary, even Ram Dass House appeared rejuvenated, the plaques beside the doors blazing in the sunlight. Looking to her left, there was no mistaking the first structure to catch her eye. Thick green grass grew up the walls and over the roof of what had probably been a Quonset hut. This had to be Tolkien House, fashioned after Hobbit dwellings and named for the author of *The Hobbit* and *The Lord of the Rings* trilogy. She delighted in the thought of a house that needed mowing instead of painting.

Then she turned around, the sight of the administration building taking her breath away. She stared in amazement. Whomever had covered the points of the star in sharp-edged metal had to have no intuitive sense. Better to have put up a yurt than this monstrosity.

"What's the matter?" Marcella asked.

"Those points. In feng shui they create what are called poison arrows and shoot destructive energy at whatever is in their path. How long have they been there?"

"Since the late sixties."

"Really?"

"Not the metal parts. Those were attached this summer. Ivy wanted to cover up the chipped concrete. Toby had a friend into metal sculpting and got a good deal on them. The artist called them sleeves. They're really sharp, too."

"Were the points originally rounded?"

"Well yes, you know, it's concrete. It would have been very expensive to replace all seven points, because the roof is somehow connected to them. I can show you around later, but we better get going now."

"So, it's a septagram," Salome said, her interest piqued. "The seven-pointed star is related to unity of Heaven and Earth and all people. And the seven directions."

"Seven?"

"North, south, east, west, above, below, within. If that's what the Ashcrofts had in mind when they first built this place, their intentions were very good. And intentions are extremely important in feng shui. Where's the chapel?"

"On the southeast corner. But it's not really a chapel.

It's a meditation space. I'll show you later," Marcella said, her eyes darting back to the doors of the administration building.

Just then, Barbara and Billie Ruth approached, rounding the south corner, Barbara huddled inside her white robe, and Billie Ruth dressed in tight black leather pants and jacket with the collar turned up.

"Yin and yang," Salome mumbled.

"Gorgeous morning," Barbara observed. "Even under the circumstances."

"Always more beautiful after a storm," Billie Ruth said with a sly smile. "Like sex after an argument."

Barbara scrunched up her nose and fanned the air in front of her face. "God! What is that stink?"

"A plumbing problem."

"Jeeze, what *didn't* happen last night?" Billie Ruth asked.

Barbara turned to Marcella. "Is it too early yet for breakfast?" The smell apparently didn't bother her appetite.

"I'm sorry. Electricity hasn't come on yet."

"So there's not even coffee?" Billie Ruth interjected.

"I'm sorry—"

Billie Ruth suddenly perked. "Is Ivy around?"

"Not yet."

Billie Ruth looked at Marcella, then at Barbara. "Hell, I can have a van over here from my bakery in forty-five minutes. People are going to be really upset if there isn't even anything hot to drink."

"I'd say go ahead and do it, but you'd better check with Ivy. Use the phone behind the desk. Press the button marked 'Big House' and you'll connect right to her."

Billie Ruth turned and trotted into the administration building.

"She's energetic this morning," Salome said.

"I think she had a yoga lesson with Roger Cane last night," Barbara remarked, her expression ironic.

"Did she tell the cops? I mean you were just interviewed, right?"

"Separately. We haven't compared notes yet."

Marcella touched Salome's arm. "We really should go. You don't want to be on the bad side of Detective Child."

"Where are you off to?"

Salome opened her coat and flashed her pajamas. "To change."

"See you later," Barbara said and turned toward the administration building, while Salome and Marcella headed for Watts House, Marcella moving at a brisk pace.

"I guess you've gotten to know Detective Child," Salome observed.

"You could say that. I think he thinks I killed Toby."

"Did you?"

Marcella stopped. "Of course not! I loved—" Marcella shut her mouth.

Salome lightly touched the sleeve of Marcella's coat. "Don't worry. Anything you say to me is in strictest confidence—you did ask me for a feng shui consultation, right?"

"Well, yes, but I never thought—"

"So I'm your feng shui consultant, and as a professional, I'm obliged to keep a client's information confidential—unless the client gives me permission to do otherwise."

"Yes, we were in love. Since we were kids. When we got older, the Ashcrofts wouldn't allow Toby and Ivy to play with us kids at the dairy. So we kinda drifted apart. Then he called a couple years ago to tell me his mother had died. He said he wanted to see me. Ivy doesn't know, she thinks I just came back because I had no place else to go."

"Surely, she must have suspected something. Love is hard to hide. And you did tell me that Toby moved you into the Playhouse."

"Toby's a generous—*was*—a generous guy. She just thought he was helping me out while I got myself together. And I started working around the place. Ivy's one of those people who can't imagine anyone in their class ever having a serious relationship with the help."

"So Ross Prenderville is *in her class*, as it were?"

"Did you see the ring she's wearing? He's a lawyer from back east. Went to *Hahvud*. Gives me the creeps. Always looks at me like I'm a piece of meat."

"Toby must have trusted him. Wasn't he Toby's attorney?"

"Just because he's good at his job doesn't mean I have to like him," she muttered.

At a desk inside the door of Watts House, a policewoman took statements from the guests. Most people sat quietly in the common room. Salome spotted Stephen and Delores. Delores looked about ready to take a piece out of someone. They must have been told to vacate Salome's room.

"Hi, Officer Swift," Marcella said.

"How ya doing, Marcella?"

"Detective Child sent me with Ms. Waterhouse. She's in room four and needs to change clothes."

When they entered the corridor, Salome said, "You *do* know everyone."

"Can't help it. I was with them for days. Ivy had me take care of them, while she took care of business."

Salome took her carryall and the clothes she'd left out into the bathroom. She figured Detective Child wouldn't want anyone making calls, but since he'd not mentioned it specifically, had been so preoccupied trashing feng shui practitioners that he'd probably forgotten, she called Phyllis on her cell phone. She turned on the faucet so Marcella wouldn't hear.

"I just met your guy."

"Good morning to you, too. Yeah, well, Gordon called earlier. To check your bona fides."

"So then you know about the death."

"No details. Like I said, he was checking you out."

"You might want to rethink this relationship, Phyllis. Emotionally, he lives up to his surname." She told Phyl about his negative response to her as a feng shui practitioner. "He acts like I'm some sort of predator."

"If it makes you feel better, the guy who broke up his best friend's marriage went to some feng shui conference and came back with instant credentials. That and some business cards made him a professional practitioner."

In the West, where credentials were all-important, people who had the money, could, after a comprehensive weekend of study, emerge with a piece of paper declaring them to be a practitioner. Salome was appalled by this. People with no experience and people with the wrong intentions could actually find clients as easily as someone like her who'd apprenticed with a master for five years before even *thinking* about going professional.

"That's like equating a Chia pet with gardening."

Phyllis suddenly laughed.

"So, how did you meet him?"

"At a banquet in San Jose—we all wore animal skins and ate with our hands. You know, typical police function."

"Got a pen and paper handy?"

"You mean you've got something for me?"

"Of course. I didn't just call to whine."

"Hold on." Salome heard her fumbling beside the bed. "Okay."

"See what you can dig up on a Carla Whitmore, Roger Cane, and Ross Prenderville. Whitmore is the victim. Roger Cane is a yoga guru who Whitmore appeared to hate—and that's something I didn't tell Child. He was too busy bad-mouthing feng shui, and I just flat forgot to mention it. Prenderville practices road rage. Got all that?"

"What's this about Prenderville?"

Salome briefly described the encounter on Highway 1.

"That's a real bitch."

"I'll say."

"No. Prenderville is one of Gordon's backers. Gordon is considering him as press secretary."

"You're joking!"

"Salome. The political stuff is on the back burner at the moment. Just don't say anything about it. Okay?"

"I better get off the phone."

"Look, I'll give Gordon a call. Tell him you're one of the good guys."

"Don't do that! He'll know I called you."

"Hey. Cool it. And you'll get to meet him socially Sunday night."

"Why? What's happening?"

"I'll tell you later."

She put the phone in her pocket, feeling she had stepped into something that should be avoided. In actuality, she had done just that, and she took a quick spit bath, focusing her energy on her feet.

Chapter 10

Most people housed south of the administration building had slept through the night. Statements given by those in houses on the north side tended to be lengthier due to the plumbing problem in Ram Dass House and subsequent invasion of nearby Watts and Leary Houses. Once their statements were taken, the guests assembled in the administration building's auditorium, where they were told to wait and not make any phone calls. No one was allowed to leave the grounds, but that didn't prevent news from leaking. Like Salome, plenty of people had cell phones and used the cover of the growing crowd to use them.

Billie Ruth's opportunism resulted in a bountiful and no doubt very expensive feed, consisting of some of the best coffee and baked goods available on the central coast.

As the auditorium filled, Salome picked up bits and pieces of information. Sometime during the night, Angela Platt, the Women's Study professor giving the workshops on building self-esteem in older women, left the institute. She'd been staying in Dilbert House, where the "rooms" were coffinlike pods similar to inexpensive accommodations in Tokyo. Billie Ruth and Barbara had also stayed in Dilbert House. Barbara said she quite enjoyed the sensation after the lights went out. Not Angela Pratt, apparently.

Roger Cane was also missing, news that disturbed Billie Ruth.

"He can't be gone!" she cried.

"Why?" Barbara coaxed.

Billie Ruth leaned forward. "Because," she said in a low voice, "we're supposed to meet tonight."

"Surely not in the coffin," Barbara quipped.

"In Dogbert House." Billie Ruth turned to Salome. "Have you been in it?"

"If you mean Dogbert House, no. In fact I've not yet been in any of the houses except Watts and Ram Dass."

"I'll let you see it for yourself. You will *not* believe it. Toby Ashcroft definitely had a perverse sense of humor." That would be natural, given that both houses were named for characters in the wildly popular cartoon strip, "Dilbert."

Salome went to refill her cup. Some of the attendees were beginning to look hostile, the chatter turning to refunds and anger at Ivy, who hadn't made an appearance yet. She couldn't blame them. Then she had an idea.

Marcella, somewhat revived by the fresh coffee, remained at the front desk.

"Is Ivy here?"

"Finally!" She nodded toward the first room in the right corridor.

Ivy and Ross Prenderville were arguing as Salome stepped through the door. "Good God, Ivy, you couldn't ask for better timing," Prenderville hissed.

"Excuse me," Salome greeted. They both froze.

"Sorry to interrupt," Salome went on quickly, "but I wanted to ask you if you'd mind if I gave a mini-workshop. To entertain the troops as it were. People are fidgety and nervous, and it might help take their minds off things."

Suddenly smiling brightly, Ivy broke away from Prenderville and joined Salome by the door. "That's a wonderful idea, Ms. Waterhouse. Yes. Just do it. I'm sure Detective Child won't mind—but I'll make sure."

Taking Salome's arm, Ivy gently steered her out into the corridor. "Ross and I were just discussing the possibility of selling the institute."

"I apologize for the interruption."

"No, no," she said, waving her hand. "In fact, you might be able to help out."

"You mean with feng shui?"

"Let's talk later. Soon as things settle down around here. All right?"

Ivy entered the office Detective Child had taken over and exited a moment later. "He says it's okay."

"Fine. When you want to talk, you know where I'll be," Salome said and went to collect her workshop paraphernalia.

A policeman in the squad car blocking access to the little bridge stopped her. She bent down and spoke to him through the window. He let her pass.

Her things were kept in a large artist's portfolio and a backpack on rollers—easy enough to cart back to the administration building.

Rather than ask and invite negative responses from the roomful of grumpy, unhappy attendees, Salome went ahead and set up at a table front and center. To use the stage would have been too intrusive. The electricity had not been restored. Many candles provided light.

On a table she positioned a portable metal easel, on which she propped a laminated Bagua, measuring 25" × 35", each gua appropriately colored. It rose above the crowd, immediately attracting attention. Below it, she placed her pointer, a wind chime, a bell, several books, a white candle, a small American flag, a brass bowl and round wooden mallet, a length of silk similar to the one she'd used to cover the mirror the previous night, a 20-mm faceted crystal, a porcelain statue of the goddess Kwan Yin, a three-foot-wide fan featuring a green dragon painted on black silk, and a three-legged rosewood frog squatting on a stack of coins. All the items could be used to attract good ch'i.

After introducing herself and briefly reiterating the fundamentals as mentioned last night in her presentation, including the definition of ch'i and how to use the Bagua, she dove right in. "First study the flow of ch'i, the energy, in your house or apartment. Do a walk-through. When you feel a block, remove the blockage. If you don't feel comfortable hanging wind chimes or crystals in the house, use color instead. Again, refer to the Bagua to determine the color to stimulate the life situation you want to improve. For instance, to increase your wealth, you would use the color purple.

"Intentions are the foundation of success with feng shui. Voice your desires and visualize the outcome. Positive thoughts and vocalizations travel through the ether and attract positive energy."

A woman in the front row immediately raised her hand. Salome nodded to her.

"In your presentation last night you said you knew how to control teenagers."

Salome laughed. "Let's say, I have some fixes. Primarily, you want your teenagers to have a sense of control. You want their room to inspire self-confidence and a feeling of security. And by 'sense of control' I don't mean that they can do whatever they want with it—tear it up, fill it with manure, or whatever. Their room should be a sanctuary.

"So, first start with the placement of the bed. The best position is at a diagonal to the door, which provides a full view of the room."

"Secondly, insist that the room be kept free of clutter. Put your foot down. This is as essential to harmony as the bed's position. Clutter and major mess equate to chaos. And teenagers have enough chaos going on in their lives both internally and externally. I'm really serious here. Clutter creates unconscious disturbances that eventually manifest in behavior. Do something about it. The combination of teenagers and messy rooms has unfortunately become a stereotype; one expects the two to go together. That mess, though, is reflecting the problems in their lives. At the same time, the parts of the room that are especially bad can tell you, as a parent, where your child is having the most trouble. Knowledge is power, and, using the Bagua, you can pinpoint those areas.

"Place the desk in the room's knowledge and spirituality gua. If that's not possible, just make certain that when they sit at the desk their back is not to the door. Being unable to see who is entering a room—for anyone—can bring about social and professional problems. If there's no other place for the desk, hang a mirror so the room's entrance will be reflected."

"Color can also bring about improvements. Let your teenager choose a color scheme from a list you provide. Light blue and green are good for study; peach and pale yellow have a calming effect and don't interfere with sleep.

"Encourage your teenager to clean the room as a way of learning about it. A thorough cleansing of any space puts you in touch with it. You learn its unique features. From that knowledge comes respect. And the more you respect your space, the more you honor yourself."

A hand shot up. Salome nodded to the woman.

"My daughter's room is covered with heavy-metal posters," the woman stated.

"The power of the color on the walls will still come through."

"Actually, there's wallpaper. And now that I think of it, it's kind of bubbly in places and starting to peel."

"Does your daughter have skin problems?"

The woman looked startled then recovered. "Well, yes. But just normal acne."

"Acne doesn't have to be normal. The wallpaper itself is like skin. When you go home, you might want to strip the walls and apply a coat of paint. In which gua is her bedroom located?"

The woman glanced down at her copy of the Bagua then back at Salome. "Family and health."

"A shade of green would be good in her room. Let her choose. Even dark green would work. You might find she'll lose interest in the heavy-metal posters, too."

"As long as she loses interest in the *music*!"

The group laughed.

"As far as locating the best place for the bedroom, the children and creativity gua is an excellent place, though some prefer knowledge and spirituality, believing their child's study habits will improve in that location."

"I have a question," someone called out.

Salome recognized the man waving his hand, but Alan Watts looked too young to have teenagers.

"Yes, Alan."

"Are some places just inherently evil?"

Salome figured Alan was thinking about the Star Institute itself and well understood his reasons for asking. But she didn't want to jump topics and lose the thread of the current discussion.

"I'll get to that in a minute, Alan. First, any more questions about teenagers?"

But "evil" had captured everyone's interest. No hand was raised, and the room had quieted.

"Let me qualify my answer, if I may. I can't give you a flat yes or no. If by 'places' you mean land, well, nature has both creative and destructive cycles, a natural part of life. Evil is a man-made concept. Now there are places to avoid building a house—say, the top of a hill, or right on the beach—places where the house will be vulnerable to the elements. So basically, no structures are inherently evil. However, bad things that happen in or near a structure can give it a sinister aspect. Walls, floors, and furniture—everything absorbs energy, especially intense energy. Buildings don't start out bad, unless the builder created the building with evil intensions. So basically, humans bring the bad energy to a place. As I said, evil itself is a human concept, not a natural occurrence in nature."

Then she spent a few minutes showing the items she'd brought and explaining their particular uses, but she was starting to drag. Her arm shook slightly as she held up the rosewood frog, fatigue melting into her muscles.

"This little fellow is a wealth icon, as you would surmise, since he's sitting on stacks of coins. He also has a string of coins in his mouth that trails down either side of his back. He's special, too, because he has only three legs and is considered very lucky. He could go just inside the front door to welcome wealth into the house or in a wealth gua in any room."

She set the frog down on the table and took a moment to regroup. "To conclude, I'll leave you with a few tips. Hang a mirror behind the stove to symbolically increase the number of burners: more burners mean more food and more food means more prosperity. The mirror also allows the cook to see who is coming up from behind. You want the cook happy, not startled by intrusions.

"Place a fan on the wall behind your desk chair." She opened the black silk fan on which was painted an undulating green dragon. "This fans you with energy and helps keep you to the task.

"Always elevate your purse. Never leave it on the floor, as this connotes a careless attitude about money.

"Position your bed so you have a full view of the room, the best position, as I mentioned earlier, being at a diagonal from the door. If you are seeking a partner allow room on both sides of the bed. By pushing one side of the bed against the wall you're eliminating access for someone else.

"I'll leave you with a favorite. Keep the lid of the toilet down. The toilet symbolizes the flushing away of finances and you want it covered so the energy is contained. You men, especially, keep that in mind."

The inevitable chuckles followed.

"Remember, ch'i is a force of nature. Thank you all."
Then she smiled playfully. "May the ch'i be with you!"
    As she started to pack up, she received the summons.
Detective Child wanted to see her in the office.

Chapter 11

☯

THE interview went more pleasantly than she'd anticipated. Maybe Phyl had talked to him or maybe he felt some gratitude that she'd keep the crowd occupied when maintaining order was essential. He questioned her more about everyone she'd come in contact with, where and when. Now, too, she remembered to mention her observations of Carla Whitmore's demeanor when Roger Cane was on stage and later after the presentations. While the tape ran, Detective Child also made notes of her observations.

"When was the last time you were here?" he asked.

"If you mean at the institute, this is my first time."

He looked surprised. "Not even in the seventies? Seems the perfect venue for someone with your interests."

"I moved to Hawaii when I was seventeen and did not return to Holyrood, as a resident, until about six years ago."

"All right. That'll do for now. You know, of course, not to leave town without checking with me first. You're free to leave."

*　　*　　*

IVY WAS STATIONED AT THE FRONT DESK, writing refund checks, having finally emerged to deal with the financial repercussions. There was a line at the desk and another by the door of those waiting for a police officer to escort them to their cars. Salome sighed. Yet another wait.

After about ten minutes, it was Salome's turn. Ivy came out from behind the desk and moved her to a quiet corner.

"I'm sorry, but I can't pay you for the weekend. Under the circumstances, there's just enough to refund these people their money. But of course, last night's and this morning's impromptu presentation provided free publicity for your business."

Salome didn't like this woman manipulating circumstances to her own end but said nothing.

"Don't get me wrong. I'm very grateful. God knows, you calmed people down—maybe even reduced the inevitable lawsuits. Anyway, your family owns Waterhouse Properties, correct?"

"My parents."

"Well, like I mentioned earlier, we are thinking of selling and are looking for the right realtor. I'm sure there's good money to be made, and I'd just as soon pass the business along to your family."

"Would you still like a feng shui consultation? I can make suggestions to increase your chances of getting a good sale."

"Let's just leave that for now, shall we? Put in a good word with your parents, okay?"

Ivy pulled away, extending a hand. "We'll be in touch."

Salome returned to the auditorium and resumed packing her feng shui items. Barbara joined her, offering to help.

"So, what was the institute like back in the seventies?" Salome asked.

"Laid back. That chapel, where they found blood this morning on the yoga mats—was really a chapel and not a meditation room," she said, not bothering to hide her scorn. "Bill and Alice Ashcroft believed in the importance of spirituality. Made all the difference in the world." She looked around, "This, this is nothing but marketing. A scam to make money off baby boomers—the aging New Agers. Relive the past, all that. I'm disappointed."

"I thought you said you liked the accommodation," Salome mentioned, while sliding the Bagua into the leather portfolio.

"Yeah, it was a kick. But that's it. A kick." She paused and then went on. "I think Ivy decided to squeeze one last penny out of this place. Spent no money on getting the old buildings in shape, on food—good grief here we are in the salad bowl of the world, and she serves limp old vegetables at that presentation dinner and *crackers*. What about cheese from their own dairy? Hell no. Not a wedge in sight.

"Last night I asked myself, What is she doing? And the answer: taking advantage of old farts like me."

"What happened to her parents?"

"Bill died in a kayaking accident about ten years ago. Weather didn't matter to him. He loved the sea—or more precisely—feeling he could conquer it. Well, who won that battle?"

"And Alice?"

"Ah, Alice. One of those gorgeous hippie chicks born to be a flower child. Long blonde hair, huge dreamy blue eyes. You'd never think of her as Ivy's mother. For that matter, you'd never even put them in the same star system—no pun intended. At least in the beginning. But she fit perfectly into Bill's plans for the Star Institute. She not only *looked* the part, but she acted the part."

Salome wrapped the three-legged frog in purple tissue. "The part of what?"

"What I suppose today you'd call an airhead. Then it was space cadet." Barbara plopped down in a chair and fumbled with the hood of her robe. "Why did I wear this?" She shook her head at her rhetorical question then answered. "I really thought something neat might happen this weekend; that I might find inner peace or something."

"Try Phyl's method—buy a chocolate bar."

Barbara cocked her head. "Hey, that would be a good name for a chocolate bar—*Inner Peace.*"

Salome added the frog to the other carefully wrapped items. "So what happened to Alice?"

"Oh yes. Well, as the institute gained notoriety and started making serious money, Bill wanted to put on a good show. He got Alice involved with various charities. She began spending more time away from here and in the company of very different people. Very rich people. Hair spray replaced flowers, high heels replaced sandals, and Paris couture took the place of jeans and Guatemalan blouses.

"When Bill saw what was happening, he tried to reel her back in. Didn't work. But Alice was a strong Catholic and didn't believe in divorce. They began their "open marriage" phase. Remember that?"

"Sure. In fact, if not in practice."

"Gradually, Alice wound back down to a simpler life again. When Bill died, she'd moved to Australia to dedicate her life to the aborigines—whether they liked it or not. She died after being bitten by a brown snake—what? Two—three years ago."

Barbara stood. "Looks like you're ready to roll."

The two women embraced. "I'm really glad to see you, Salome. Believe it or not, I think you may have changed my mind about feng shui. Listening to you today made me think there may be something about it worth considering."

"And Barbara, you really do look terrific. What's your secret?"

"Botox."

"What?"

"Botox. It's quite simple really. I get these injections at a spa in San Jose. They contain a tiny dose of botulism."

"Yikes!"

"Don't knock it until you've tried it. It really works to get rid of wrinkles. As you can see."

DRIVING BACK TO HOLYROOD, SALOME FELT anaerobic; too much time in the lowlight making her eyes sensitive. Brilliant shafts of sunlight shot through the spaces between the scudding gray clouds. Most of the way home, she squinted at the road, but the warmth was more than welcome.

The details of the past seventeen–eighteen hours, the people, their propinquity to events cluttered her mind, but she felt too tired to put everything in order. One thing did separate itself from the random images and stay with her. She felt that sadness blanketed the institute, as if the natural environment was responding to some seriously bad intentions.

On the way home, she stopped at the dry cleaners, where Kim, the proprietress, assured her the robe would be good as new in several days. The two women talked for a few minutes. Kim mentioned that business had recently picked up since she hung the black and gold wind chime above the cash register, as Salome had suggested.

HOME HAD NEVER LOOKED AND FELT SO good. In the foyer, though burdened with her bags, she stood motionless for a long moment, just breathing in the peaceful, harmonious atmosphere and the prevailing scent of sandalwood. Maybe she would position herself at the center of the gentle aromatic web and not leave until Thanksgiving, or Christmas, or ever.

Like a good host, ShiShi trotted into the foyer and loudly voiced a greeting. She put her bags down and picked up the kitty, her own "protective lion."

"In future, I shall take more care before accepting invitations to weekend seminars."

Still, the Star Institute certainly merited a chapter in her private "murder house" studies.

She kissed the soft black and white furry face, and ShiShi became instant putty.

She carried the hanging bag into the laundry room. She hung up the unworn cassock-like robe to air out then stripped, and dumped everything else into the washer, wanting to rid her clothes of any accumulated bad energy.

After a shower and vigorous shampoo, she felt revitalized. She dressed in comfortable sweats and went to her study. Inserting a tape of Taiko drums in the boom box, she unpacked the rolling backpack, placing the tissue-wrapped feng shui enhancements in their respective spaces in the built-in cabinet.

Turning the volume down, she then checked her phone messages, half-hoping for an update on Mah's whereabouts from Jude. But there were no messages of any significance. Thinking of Mah served as a reminder to reinforce the protection energies, especially in the helpful people guas, and check basic security.

She pulled a notebook and pen from the top drawer of her desk and was just about to prepare a "to do" list, when the phone rang.

"Good eye, Salome," Phyllis greeted.

"Phyl?"

"Your suggestion about a link between Carla Whitmore and Roger Cane turned out to be right on."

Whitmore's sister, Phyllis said, had been married to Tel Becker, the publisher of Roger Cane's books and videos.

"And Becker was a wife beater. Couple years back, after a separation, the sister was found beaten to death, and Becker was the prime suspect. The case went to trial. Roger Cane appeared as a character witness for the defense. Anyway, Becker was acquitted. All very O. J. After the trial, Becker put more promotion money into Cane's books and videos.

"Then Becker died in a house fire—in itself mysterious—and Carla Whitmore started writing flaky letters to

New Age publications, smearing Roger Cane in an attempt to prevent him from getting a new publisher, making it her mission to ruin his career.

"No offense to you, Salome, but his appearance at the Star Institute was a good indication that Whitmore's campaign was working. His publicist dropped him, and he was having trouble getting classy gigs."

For that matter, Salome's publicist hadn't been impressed with her decision to appear at the institute. But the timing of the event coinciding with her return to Holyrood for the winter had been a determining factor. Besides, she'd thought it would be fun.

"Anyway, there's an APB out for Cane. Shouldn't be too hard to find him. He's got a rental car and it's unlikely he'll make it too far. My guess is he lacks the necessary criminal instincts."

After they'd rung off, Salome fixed a tuna sandwich, which she ate with her favorite Route 11 Dill Pickle potato chips made in Middletown, Virginia. She'd shipped a carton to Holyrood before leaving Georgetown.

Somewhere around 9 o'clock, after the house had been cleaned, her second wind petered out. She stretched out on the new bed, intending to "test it out" for a few minutes before showering and finishing up with a quiet read. But her body had other ideas, and when the phone woke her, morning light filtered through the shutters at the window.

Chapter 12

☯

THE yellow and white twenty-bedroom Victorian lodge that dominated the twelve-acre Otter Haven Resort had been in the Waterhouse family for nearly a century. Salome's parents, Reginald and Satomi Waterhouse, owned and managed the property, which included twelve tiny storybook cottages, and had done so since receiving it as a wedding present from Reggie's parents, Joshua and Salome. During those fifty-six years, they had raised four daughters and a niece in the north wing of the lodge. In the early days, Satomi managed the day-to-day operations, while Reggie built moderate-income houses around the central coast area and ran a real estate business, Waterhouse Properties.

Nothing much ever changed here, despite natural disasters or social upheaval. Otter Haven, with its splendid east, south, and western vistas, huge cypress trees, gracefully bent by time and weather, the stately Victorian lodge, the stone cottages, with their mullioned windows, rounded doors, and features attractive to elves and fairies had endured as a result of a special blend of excellent location and the character of the owners. Reggie and Satomi Waterhouse treated the property as sacred space, the lodge like a temple.

Though a wealthy family, no job was beneath any family member, whether it was weeding the daffodil and tulip beds that hugged the cottages or cleaning toilets in the guest rooms.

Salome picked up her pace when she reached the brooding, neglected house just outside the gate to Otter Haven. Damon O'Kelly and his yard art, wooden statues of odd beasts and local politicos—and with some, combinations of the two—entertained tourists and kept Damon's bank account pumped up. As Salome and her sisters believed, he'd been born without the part of the brain that encourages good behavior. Rather than put him away, the O'Kelly family chose to put him to use. The O'Kellys hated the Waterhouses, and stationing Damon on a property they owned right beside the gate to the popular resort seemed ideal. Of course, the plan backfired. Instead of driving people away, after the initial shock of him, the guests were amused. Then, after the first sale, Damon found his calling and wouldn't have left, even if the O'Kellys themselves decided to move him. He'd been in the dilapidated house, his sculptures like strange growths in the weedy yard, since Salome's childhood. Whenever he spotted one of Reggie and Satomi's daughters, he'd race to his fence and taunt them. He'd never done physical harm—other than scorch their ears with obscenities. Rather than create more trouble with lawsuits, the Waterhouses either ignored him or treated him like the damaged soul he was, occasionally voicing a pleasant greeting. Damon wasn't going anywhere, and besides, he was probably the least troublesome member of the vindictive O'Kelly clan.

The screen door banged, and Damon shot down the steps and into the yard. He wore a peach-colored leather jacket with linebacker pads in the shoulders, a style favored by women decades ago. One side was faded from the hours he spent outside sculpting. He screamed something incomprehensible.

"Good afternoon to you, too, Damon," Salome intoned.

He blinked. A pleasant greeting sometimes left him speechless. Then he grabbed a tall block of redwood he'd been working on and carried it to the fence. He'd fashioned a police officer, identifiable as such by the uniform and hat. He'd left some hairy bark on the face just under the nose. The face was startling in it's precision. No mistake, the figure was Phyllis.

"Five hundred do-lar-es, oh oh. Do-lar-es, oh oh oh oh!" He sang out, a Damon O'Kelly rendition of "Volare," and swung the sculpture in an awkward dance, his arms wrapped around the waist. She hurried on, before he got the notion to gross her out by humping the block of wood.

Salome passed through the gate, leaving Damon looking disappointed.

Without mentioning anything specific, her mother had called inviting her over and said they'd be in the dining room, which was unusual. Unless it was a very slow day, her parents would not normally take up a table that could be used by a guest. From the number of cars she could see in the lot on the far east side, plenty of people were partaking of the resort's popular Sunday brunch.

Salome moved along the flagstone path that wound around the back of the lodge and passed under a favorite cypress, its branches spread out twenty feet on each side. She felt lighter, and her pace picked up as it always did here. Never in her travels had she experienced a duplicate of Otter Haven's energy.

She walked up the south side steps to the veranda that girdled the lodge along the front, delicate latticework joining the struts to the overhang. A couple, bundled in matching red jackets, strolled down the gentle slope of thick green grass that led to the cliff's edge. The tide was out, and she reasoned they were headed for Otter Cove, accessible by the wooden stairs that zigzagged down to the beach.

She opened the beveled-glass front doors and entered the lodge. Straight ahead and across a black and red oriental carpet was the polished mahogany reception desk. To the right was a large common area furnished with groupings of sofas, chairs, and coffee tables, positioned beside windows and in front of the large fireplace. Farther on was an alcove covered with bookshelves where guests could borrow all sorts of paperback novels and board games. And beyond that area was the family residence.

Salome's attention was drawn to the dining room on the left. Her mother had already decorated for Thanksgiving, each table featuring ikebana in autumn colors and unusual combinations of flora—tiny pumpkins with an orchid, brilliant red and yellow maple leaves posed with flax lilies curved into half-bows. Two huge *La Rouge* pumpkins were stationed on either side of the dining room's fireplace and paired with white pumpkins.

Even though she sat with her back to the entrance, Salome's mother turned and waved as Salome surveyed the room. Good radar, Salome thought absently. She smiled and hurried toward the table. Her smile dropped when she saw her parents' brunch partners: Ivy Ashcroft and Ross Prenderville.

Prenderville stood and pulled out a chair for Salome. She met her father's blue eyes but read little there. His poker face rarely revealed anything. She bent down and kissed her mother's smooth cheek, wrinkles kept at bay by a cream made of crushed pearls, which seemed a lot healthier than Barbara Boatwright's wrinkle-retardant of choice. The gray in her hair was kept to a minimum by years of clean living, a forgiving nature, and a refusal to worry or take anything personally.

Her scent, if bottled, could have made her a fortune. In the wonderful aroma of Ivory soap, pine incense from the altar where she made her morning prayers, and oil of white ginger, Salome always glimpsed, though fleetingly, a perfect world. Of course, on anyone else but her mother, the scent wouldn't have been the same.

Today Satomi wore a cream silk blouse and a black angora cardigan and black slacks, baroque pearls at her ears and the ring finger of her right hand. Her father had on his normal attire, which changed little, no matter how many polo shirts and nice trousers Satomi bought him— a cable knit sweater over a denim work shirt and jeans.

In contrast, Ivy wore a bright red sweater dress, torques of twisted silver and gold at her neck and wrist, matching earrings, and that mammoth diamond that never failed to catch the eye. Salome recalled Barbara's tale about Ivy's parents. Something of her mother's fashionable years had stuck with her daughter.

Salome, in clean gray fleece, might have felt under dressed had this not been home. She'd scrubbed and polished this very floor, cleaned and polished this very table, even the underside, and each chair. Besides, her mother hadn't said anything about dressing up. She wore her long mane in a single braid that trailed down her back.

"I guess you're surprised to see us," Ivy remarked after the general greetings.

"Get yourself a plate, Mei," Satomi said.

"Maybe later," Salome replied and squeezed her mother's hand. Sitting beside a man whose reckless impatience could have gotten her killed soured her appetite.

"I'd planned to talk to my parents first," Salome said to Ivy and glanced at her father.

"We need to get the ball rolling," Ross said, slicing into a crab cake that looked divine, a creation of her mother's—about the only thing she prepared for the brunch any more. "We'll be talking to several realtors, of course, but since we know you, we wanted your father to have first crack."

"What's the hurry?"

The question seemed to startle both Ivy and Ross. Satomi concentrated on her lunch. Reggie sipped from a goblet that appeared to be filled with tomato juice. Salome knew it was Bloody Mary mix and wondered if he'd gotten vodka in it before Satomi noticed.

Ivy put down her fork and patted her lips with a white linen napkin. "After what's happened, I don't see the institute as a going concern. Besides, I really know nothing about the hospitality business, and I'm not an educator. The institute's functions just don't jibe with my interests or expertise. Yes, I could probably find someone to run it, but why? With Toby gone, the place is just one big reminder of what I've lost. So, the sooner it's sold the better. I'm more a city person anyway, and the place is just too remote."

"But you are keeping the dairy, right?" Reggie asked.

"It's a good income. Always has been."

"Would you be adverse to development of the parcels?"

"Once I sell, it's gone as far as I'm concerned. Whoever buys it can do whatever they please. I'm not an environmentalist, I'm a realist."

Salome thought about what Barbara had told her yesterday, especially the mention of a scam.

Reggie, Ross, and Ivy discussed options, including the possibility of putting together a syndicate. Her father hinted that Waterhouse Properties might be interested in buying the property outright. Ivy took a small notebook and a gold pen from her purse and jotted notes.

Ross left the table and returned with a medley of desserts: a wedge of cheesecake, a piece of chocolate cake, a large slice of coconut cake. Desserts came from Billie Ruth's bakery—no one in the area came close to the quality of her food, and Satomi wisely offered her guests an assortment every Sunday and at high tea on Wednesday afternoons.

Ivy declined Ross's offer to share dessert.

"Only one requirement," Satomi announced. She'd said nothing since Salome had been at the table. Everyone turned to her as if seeing her for the first time.

"Requirement for what, Mrs. Waterhouse?" Ivy asked pleasantly.

Reggie gave his wife a wary look. Salome was amused, wondering what sort of bomb her mother was going to drop.

"If you want to be listed with Waterhouse Properties," Satomi said and leaned forward putting both hands on either side of her plate, "then we must first see the results of a feng shui report. Once that has been supplied, we'll be in a better position to make a firm decision."

A silence dropped. Noise from the nearby tables seemed to stop at their chairs. Satomi looked at Ivy and then at Ross. "You do want to sell for the best price? And quickly?"

Ivy glanced at Ross. "Well of course."

"Then we require a feng shui report, which my daughter can provide."

"No offense, Mrs. Waterhouse, but real estate is real estate. Feng shui doesn't make a bit of difference when there's a market." Ross pushed his dessert plate to one side. He'd eaten about half of each one.

Reggie shifted in his seat and cleared his throat. "Donald Trump uses feng shui consultants, son, and I think he knows a thing or two about real estate."

Satomi smiled sweetly. "Savvy sellers use feng shui."

Ivy reached over and touched Ross's arm. "Mrs. Waterhouse is right, Ross. I think a feng shui consultation would be a good thing. In fact, we talked about that, didn't we, Salome?"

Ross looked smug. "Fine. But we still have that meeting with"—he pulled a card out of his jacket and glanced at it perfunctorily—"O'Kelly Realty."

Another log fueled the fire of Salome's dislike for the man; Ross must have learned about the feud—not that it wasn't common knowledge—and was playing one family against the other. Of course there was nothing illegal about such a practice, and she had to admit it was a shrewd way to jump up the price—let Waterhouse and O'Kelly fight it out, try and outbid each other—but she didn't have to like it.

"How about coming over this afternoon, Salome? What will it take? One, two hours?"

"More like three."

"You know the O'Kellys?" Ross asked Reggie.

For Ross, the timing was bad. Reggie's attention had suddenly shifted to something or someone behind his wife and daughter. "Good heavens!"

He pushed his chair back and rose. Salome and Satomi turned in their seats.

Phyllis and Gordon Child approached the table.

When they arrived, Phyllis gave Reggie a hug and a kiss, moved to Satomi and gave her a respectful peck on the cheek, then squeezed Salome's shoulder. Moving back beside Gordon, she regarded the upturned faces with such benevolence that for a moment Salome thought she was about to bestow a blessing. Instead, she made introductions. Ivy and Ross, of course, knew Gordon but not Phyllis.

Salome sensed the importance of the occasion—the equivalent of bringing a new love home to meet the parents. And though Phyllis always referred to them as Aunt Satomi and Uncle Reggie, they were like parents, her own having died when she was a child. Reggie had taken in his brother's daughter, and he and Satomi tried to raise Phyl as one of their own. While Reggie could easily pass as Phyl's father, there was no mistaking the absence of a genetic bond with Satomi. Maybe because of that Phyllis had always been closer to her uncle.

Phyllis looked as if she'd been feng shuied from head to foot. And maybe she had. The new, softer, highlighted hairstyle, makeup, the turquoise and gold silk shantung dress all suited her beautifully.

"We've just been to church," Phyllis said, after the introductions.

Reggie and Satomi gave no sign that this was in any way unusual. Salome smiled, also not giving anything away, not asking, for instance, if the church was still standing. Unless she snuck in late at night when no one was around to see her, Phyllis hadn't seen the inside of Holyrood church since their grandfather's funeral in the 1980s.

"What a charming church it is," Gordon commented. To Reggie he added, "Phyllis told me your father built it."

"Along with the storybook cottages that give our village its unique character."

"After lunch I'm giving Gordon the tour."

"Look," Ross interjected and stood up. "Why don't you sit here? Ivy and I need to get going."

"I think that table by the fireplace," Phyllis said. "But thanks."

"Let me see about clearing it off for you, honey," Satomi said, and the three of them moved off.

Reggie shook hands with Ross, and they agreed to talk later.

"I'd better make sure it's all right for you to come to the institute," Ivy said and went over to speak to Gordon.

She returned to the table, smiling broadly. "The big guy says yes."

Big guy? Salome thought.

They set a time for a 3 o'clock consultation.

When she and her father were alone, Salome said, "You know what Prenderville's doing."

"Christ, I'm not senile, Mei. Soon as the bid reaches the obscene level, I'll bow out. Francis O'Kelly doesn't have the kind of money it would take. But just to keep it out of my hands, he'd make up the difference by putting his other properties up as collateral. And if that land doesn't turn around, he'll be up shit creek. And that's when I come back with the paddle—so to speak. He'll end up having to sell some of the properties down in the village, maybe even the shopping center—which I could care less about. But those village properties, that's what I want."

And she knew as well as he did that Francis O'Kelly wouldn't be able to resist. For years her father had been trying to get parcels in the village that the O'Kelly clan owned and leased to various restaurants, art galleries, and beachwear stores. Francis was the current patriarch and ten years younger than Reggie; time, though, had not diluted the venom that coursed through the O'Kelly veins.

Reggie and Salome both smiled as Satomi approached. Then her father said conspiratorially, "Let's not talk to your mother about this, all right?"

"Sure, Dad."

Not that it mattered. Satomi thought the feud with the O'Kellys was a waste of time and effort and had chosen to ignore it. She had to know Reggie's intentions but would not intrude too much. However Reggie chose to handle business that involved the O'Kellys was his business.

"Phyllis has never looked better," Satomi said as she joined them. She turned to Salome. "Now go get yourself something to eat, honey."

"I'm really not all that hungry, Mom."

Reggie watched Phyllis and Gordon at the buffet table. "When was the last time you saw her in a dress?"

Salome shook her head. "I didn't even know she had one."

Satomi looked out the window and said contemplatively, "A piece of property would be a nice wedding gift, don't you think, Reggie dear?"

Then before she even realized what she was doing, Salome blurted, "How about the Perfume?"

Chapter 13

THE *Perfume* was, of course, shorthand for the Perfume Mansion, Holyrood's showpiece, a magnificent Spanish Revival home Salome had inherited from her grandfather. The day the will was read marked the end of a close, sisterly relationship she had had with Phyllis. Where Salome felt uncomfortable and never liked the grand old house, Phyllis adored the place, as everyone, her grandfather especially, knew. Phyllis blamed Salome for Joshua Waterhouse's choice.

Then last year, Salome had offered to share the rent from the mansion with her cousin. But Phyllis's pride and a stubborn streak resulted in a negative response, and the property continued to stand between them, casting a shadow.

"It's always felt like a burden," Salome explained. "And we all know how Phyllis feels about it."

"Maybe we should wait for an actual wedding announcement," Reggie remarked dryly.

"Has Phyllis said anything to you?" Salome asked her mother.

"She doesn't have to. Just look at her!"

"I didn't see a ring or anything," Salome said, glancing over at the table by the fireplace.

"You didn't notice the bulge in his pocket? Could be a ring box."

"That's probably a gun, Mother. He's a homicide detective."

Satomi's eyes widened. "Really! My, my, they do have a lot in common."

"Good God, Satomi. Phyllis puts a dress on, and you immediately put her at the altar!"

"You didn't see her glow?"

"The sun is shining, my dear." Reggie then moved around the table and carefully bestowed a kiss on his wife's cheek and squeezed her hand. Then he left the dining room.

Salome almost laughed. He couldn't see "the glow" despite emitting it himself.

She finally helped herself to a slice of Key Lime pie to occupy her while waiting for Phyllis and Gordon. She was curious what they'd say on their way out. Returning to the table, she expected to discuss plans for Thanksgiving. But Satomi had other things on her mind. "Now that your father's gone we can discuss this latest murder. I heard you were in on the discovery of the body."

Reggie never could understand his wife's interest in what he considered to be "the macabre." But to Satomi, death was not something to fear, was simply one of many changes on life's eternal path. Murder just made it more interesting.

"That was fast!"

"Nothing slows news of murder, Mei. You know that."

She went through the events quickly, adding Gordon Child's participation but leaving out his distaste for feng shui practitioners. Nor did she bring up his political aspirations. That was for Phyllis to tell, if and when she wanted to.

"I think Ivy Ashcroft would like the investigation to be as quick and quiet as possible."

Satomi glanced toward Phyllis's table. "But not Gordon Child." Then Satomi abruptly rose. "Excuse me, dear."

"Sure, Mom."

Salome finished her pie, thinking of her mother's sudden insight. If this was Child's final case, and if he was planning a political career, keeping out of the news wouldn't be to his benefit. Was it possible that Child would prefer the investigation to drag on, to keep his name out there as long as possible? And lucky Gordon, he had not one but *two* murders to exploit. She almost felt sorry for Ivy Ashcroft.

Then she saw them moving past the window: the cameraman and the well-known broadcast journalist from a San Jose news station, her hair and makeup perfect, dressed in a stylish suit. Satomi must have spotted them, and that was why she'd left the table so suddenly.

The question was, of course, who had called them? Or were they simply tracking Child's movements like paparazzi?

Satomi had managed to lock the front doors before the TV crew reached them. She hurried over to Phyllis and Gordon. A moment later, Gordon and Satomi left together, the doors were unlocked, and Gordon conducted an interview in the sitting room on the other side of reception.

"So much for a quiet lunch," Salome said when Phyllis came up to the table.

Phyllis smiled. "Guess I'd better get used to it."

Salome stood up.

"You going to be around tonight?" Phyllis asked.

"Probably. No hot dates in my immediate future."

"Come down to the Beach Bistro around seven." Phyllis said then left the dining room. This must be what she'd been referring to when she mentioned yesterday that Salome would "get to meet him socially Sunday night."

Satomi stood in front of the reception desk where she could keep an eye on both the dining and sitting rooms.

So far, the diners hadn't been disturbed, but a crowd was forming near Gordon and the TV crew.

"Let us know about the feng shui at the institute," Satomi said and hugged her oldest daughter. A moment later, Salome slipped out the door. She'd heard enough press conferences to know Gordon wasn't really divulging anything new, though unlike others she had seen, he certainly seemed to be enjoying himself. For that matter, so was her radiant cousin.

DURING THE DRIVE BACK TO THE STAR Institute, Salome reconfigured her thoughts, now centering on the task ahead and the people involved, then specifically on Ross Prenderville.

Feng shui had taught her the importance of eliminating negative thoughts. The principle was simple: like attracts like. By giving off negative energy, negative energy comes right back. It had to be eliminated, replaced with the positive thought, much like the principle of giving love to those you hate.

Basically, it was a matter of controlling emotions, hate being one of the most vicious and negative of all. And Salome was struggling now, fighting this building hatred for Ross Prenderville. He had brought her family into his game, something she found intolerable. And though she knew her father could handle this new development, there was always a chance that Reggie's plan would backfire— even though the O'Kellys were not known for rational behavior.

Keeping her eyes on the road, she allowed her thoughts to drift into the past. One item in particular appeared. It was something that her parents didn't know she knew. Her paternal grandmother and namesake had told her the story one very bad night when she herself had been wounded by the O'Kellys' hatred. Though the years had diluted the incident to its raw components, the feeling of that night never changed, like a scent that invokes a vivid memory of a person or place. And this feeling was the equivalent of a moldering body.

She and Michael O'Kelly, the only good seed to come out of their genetic briar patch, had been secretly dating for several months. Just before Christmas in their senior year of high school, they'd gone to a secluded beach to park. Fortunately both were still fully dressed when Michael's older brother yanked open the door and threw Michael on the ground there to commence beating him. Michael's father, Brian, had grabbed Salome by the hair and dragged her out of the car and into his own. He drove her to Otter Haven, where a party for local business owners was in progress. Again, taking her by the hair, he pulled her into the lodge's dining room and shocked the guests to silence with a bitter and cruel rodomontade about Salome's loose morals and the degenerate nature of anyone with Japanese blood.

A young Hector Gonzaga had escorted his mother, then owner of the Beach Bistro, to the party. He'd been the first in the stunned group to act. Salome couldn't remember who had helped Hector, but the two men had gotten Brian O'Kelly out of the lodge before Reggie Waterhouse had had a chance to kill him. She remembered that her mother hadn't moved, that her expression of quiet resolve never changed. Then her grandmother had scooped her up and shuttled her back to her house, the very house in which Salome now lived.

In the living room, her grandmother Waterhouse had wrapped her in a green and gold silk shawl and hugged her while she sobbed.

"Why did Mother just stand there? She hates me!"

"Never ever fault your mother, Salome. If she'd batted an eye, or given a sign, your father, my son, would have killed Brian O'Kelly with his bare hands. Make no mistake O'Kelly was lucky tonight. So was your father."

"I never want to see any of them again."

"I'm going to tell you a story, something you must

never repeat. Not to Phyllis or your sisters—or anyone, for that matter."

She then left the sofa and poured two brandies. Once settled again, she began.

"Before your parents married, when Reg and Satomi were courting, Brian O'Kelly got wind of the relationship. He was always on the lookout for some way to harm Reggie, so he made a trip to Salinas to see what sort of woman had captured my son's heart. Well, he saw her all right. I don't know if he'd have gone to such lengths as he did if she hadn't been so beautiful. This was after Pearl Harbor, you see, and just at the time when Japanese Americans were being sent to internment camps.

"O'Kelly went to Satomi's parents, saying he'd fix it so they wouldn't suffer in the internment camps if they sold Satomi to him. She would have been installed in O'Kelly's house, and being a piece of property she wouldn't have had to endure the camps—just O'Kelly. Well, obviously, they were appalled and declined, which enraged him.

"You have to understand that in those days Japanese— and Chinese—women were often treated as chattel, a possession to be bartered for. Anyway, Brian O'Kelly, who had never even spoken to your mother, who she didn't know from Adam, waited for an opportunity. One night after the Japanese families had been rounded up and taken to the Salinas rodeo grounds, Brian O'Kelly bribed a guard. He entered the grounds and after spotting Satomi told her he had a message from Reggie. She followed him outside. He took her to his car and started to rip off her clothes. Fortunately, the same guard had been watching and rushed out and stopped Brian before he could do any real damage."

By now, Salome's eyes were dry and concentrated on her grandmother's face. And she wanted to find Brian O'Kelly and kill him herself.

"Before the family was shipped to the camp in Poston, Arizona, I received a letter from Satomi. The letter detailed what had happened to her, but she was afraid Brian would boast to Reggie that he'd actually raped her, or even that she'd consented. Her fear was that your father would be so provoked that he just might kill Brian. Brian had the sense to keep his mouth shut—after all, there was a witness.

"So, like I say, don't ever fault your mother; she has the family's best interests at heart."

The next day Michael O'Kelly had been sent east to a boys' school, ushered out of town by his own family before he could even speak on his own behalf, before he could even say good-bye to Salome.

After the New Year, Salome chose to spend the final semester of her senior year in Honolulu with one of her mother's sisters and her husband. She did not return to Holyrood to live until six years ago when her grandmother died and Salome bought her house, deciding to split her time between both coasts.

Chapter 14

SALOME turned off the highway and began the climb on the narrow road, purposefully early. Not a problem, as she could walk around, familiarize herself with the exteriors. And maybe Marcella was available, as Salome was interested in seeing the Playhouse.

Salome stopped at the crest of the hill, the Big House on her right, the Playhouse nestled in the trees to the left. Directly ahead, Ashcroft Dairy was tucked into the green folds of the valley. At times, she imagined, this view would be more compelling than that of the sea to the west. Cows grazed in the valley and on the hills. The road wound down through the pasture to the buildings of the dairy itself. It appeared to be a world removed, a pastoral place conducive to quiet contemplation.

She had just started around the back of the Big House, attracted by what looked like a terraced garden, when she heard her name.

Marcella stood on the porch of the Playhouse and waved. Salome acknowledged the greeting and made her way across the gravel to a tiny lawn. A bottlebrush tree, sporting abundant red blooms that gave the tree its name, hid most of the porch. The tree needed to be cut back to allow light into the house—she could just barely see the front window. At the same time, the tree probably kept the local hummingbirds in nectar, that in itself very good ch'i.

"Have you come for a consultation?" Marcella asked, her eyes bright with anticipation.

"I have. And since Ivy's not home yet, I might as well have a look at the Playhouse."

"Super! Come in, come in."

The hardwood floors creaked from the rattling front door with its oval pane of etched glass, down the hall past a tiny kitchen on the left, and on into the living room, where a worn carpet subdued the sound. At the end of the line from the front door was a futon couch with a black and red cover.

French doors, which stood open, led to a crumbling concrete patio.

"I've just been cleaning, airing the place out," Marcella explained. Salome went to the doors, furniture polish and disinfectant still discernible in the fresh air.

A wrought-iron table and chairs, the white paint streaked with rust, was centered among terra cotta pots of bright red and purple geraniums. But the flowers were overpowered by the collection of pumpkins and jack-o'-lanterns, many beginning to rot.

"The pumpkins look ready for the compost heap, Marcella. This is your fame and reputation gua. It's not a good idea tó have rotten produce here—or anyplace else, for that matter.

"They remind me of Toby. I hate to throw them out. He carved those jack-o'-lanterns, you know."

To Salome's way of thinking, they brought to mind Toby's moldering corpse. The deteriorating pumpkins spilled over into the relationship gua. On the other side of the patio, in the wealth gua, a sturdy oak tree grew. While it didn't alleviate the accumulating bad ch'i in fame and relationships, it held a promise of sound finances.

Turning back into the living room, Salome was stunned

by the sight of the fireplace. The brickwork extended all the way to the ceiling and had been fashioned into a sharp wedge that jutted out about a foot from its position in the corner. In the overall layout of the house, this was the family and health gua, and from what she'd seen so far, was the dominant feature of the house. The wedge was aimed at the relationship gua, where the sofa was angled.

"Is this the original fireplace?"

"Sure. Friends of the Ashcrofts had one just like it in their house in Carmel. Apparently, Mr. Ashcroft made some calculations and said it was aligned with one of the points of the star at the admin building. He liked to do stuff like that—didn't make sense to anyone but him."

"Well, it needs softening. Maybe you could hang a plant with trailing vines and rounded leaves in front of it."

Marcella guided Salome through the rest of the house. On the east side were two bedrooms separated by a tiny bathroom. The original wallpaper, featuring baby chicks, lambs, and calves covered the walls of the bedroom in the helpful people/travel gua of the house and was where Toby Ashcroft stored spare computer equipment. The bathroom, in the children/creativity position, had not been converted to adult use and featured a small bathtub, the sink, and toilet low to the ground. The bedroom in the relationship gua had been decorated with adults in mind— or rather, Toby Ashcroft's concept of "adult." The ceiling was covered with a map of the stars. The double bed stood on a platform in the center of the north wall and faced a large television enclosed inside an armoire. Lightweight curtains hung at the two east windows. The room was stuffy, the bed neatly made. On one side of the armoire was a shelf crammed with science fiction paperbacks.

"I just come in here to get dressed," Marcella said, looking uncomfortable.

"Where do you sleep?"

"On the couch in the living room. It pulls out into a bed."

"Given that the wedge from the fireplace is aimed right at that couch, you'd be better off sleeping in here."

She shrugged. "I don't know . . . it feels so lonely."

"You're comfortable on the couch?"

"Not really. Can't say I've been comfortable anywhere since Toby died. I kind of feel like my days are numbered."

"How do you mean?" Salome asked sharply.

"Like I won't be here much longer. In this house, I mean."

She was right, of course, since Ivy planned to sell everything except the dairy.

The kitchen being the first room in the house suggested that those who lived here would automatically think of food as soon as they entered, which could lead to weight problems.

"While we've got the good weather, would you show me around the grounds?"

"Sure." Marcella pulled a jacket off the coat tree beside the door. She looked anxious. "Maybe you can pick up something at the pumpkin patch, you know what I mean?"

"About Toby's death?"

"Well, yes."

They moved off and stopped in front of the Big House, looking west. Now in full daylight she had a better picture of the institute and focused on the immense sharp edged wedges radiating from the administration building.

Straight ahead, the east point was aligned with the left side of the Big House, the maleficent energy hitting the knowledge/spirituality gua on both floors.

Salome turned and pointed to the left side of the house. "What rooms are there?"

"That's Toby's bedroom. Above it is a storage room."

Salome turned her attention to the northeast point of the star, the Playhouse in a direct line, the shrubs and trees providing a buffer. However, the fireplace with its wedge design reconfigured the bad energy, sorely affecting the relationship gua of the living room, Marcella's bed particularly, and the property as a whole.

The north point was aimed directly at the front of Ram Dass House, where yellow crime scene tape added an eerie homily: POLICE LINE DO NOT CROSS to the BE HERE NOW admonition.

Then there was Watts House in line with the northwest point, and farther on, the pumpkin patch and the place where the stand had been positioned. To be precise, though, Salome thought, the eucalyptus trees bordering the road would absorb much of the disturbing energy before it reached that corner of the patch. Watts House, she reasoned, had been lucky not to suffer more than the onslaught of unexpected guests, the stink, and general disruption. Of course, "disruption" was the hallmark of a poison arrow.

Leary House was fortunately out of the path of a poisoned arrow. She was curious, though, and asked Marcella about the white clapboard structure.

"But for the murals, Peter Max–type stuff from the sixties, it's kind of ordinary. Not what you'd think from the plaque that says 'Turn on, tune in, drop out.' There are chairs and sofas in the common room, communal rest rooms, simple sleeping rooms."

"I haven't seen much of the south side," Salome said.

The two women walked down the gentle slope, stopping first outside the chapel, situated in a line with the southeast point of the star. As it did at Ram Dass House, crime scene tape stretched across the narrow front door. The structure looked to be no bigger than a wooden bathhouse with slits of yellow glass at about three-foot intervals.

"There's a skylight," Marcella said, "and when the sun shines it's all yellowy and peaceful inside—or it used to be anyway."

As they approached Dilbert House, in between the southeast and south points of the star, Marcella said, "Dilbert was originally Kesey House, after the author Ken

Kesey. You see, Mrs. Ashcroft named the houses on the north after her favorite contemporary philosophers. Mr. Ashcroft chose his favorite writers. Toby and his dad didn't get along, so Toby didn't care about changing the names when he started the retreat for techies."

"Why didn't he change the names of the north side houses?"

"Oh, he left those alone out of respect for his mom. And he adored J. R. R. Tolkien's books; that was always his favorite house anyway."

Beside the front door of Dilbert House was a square of clear plastic. Outlined in black was the following message:

PREDICTION 8
In the future, there will be a huge market for technology products that help workers goof off and still get paid.

—SCOTT ADAMS
The Dilbert Future

"I know about the pods in Dilbert House, but what's in Dogbert?"

"Let's see if the door's still unlocked."

A moment later, they entered what looked like an office with cubicles scattered around the main room. Salome stepped inside the cubicle closest to the door and laughed. Fitted like a workstation, the small area contained a desk and chair, hooks for clothes, and, on the floor, a length of thick foam made up with sheets, blankets, and a pillow. A white robe with TFT embroidered on the front pocket hung from one of the hooks. Salome now understood what Billie Ruth had been talking about when she observed that Dilbert House reflected Toby's sense of humor.

"The techies loved these accommodations. Remember the housing shortage during the computer boom? So many people couldn't find a place to live. Some slept in their cars, some on buses that ran all night. And some would curl up under their desks."

Marcella touched the foam mattress with her toe. "Actually, they're the most comfortable beds of any of the houses. Used to come with laptops, but of course, Ivy sold them. If it wouldn't have cost money, she would definitely have changed this house. I think it kind of embarrassed her. The bathrooms are nice, though."

"What was the former name of this house?" Salome asked when they were outside, having noticed holes by the door where a plaque had been removed. In its place,

For the first time ever, it's a great time to be a geek.

—JON KATZ
Geeks

was painted like stylistic graffiti.

"Kerouac House, after Jack Kerouac."

The round red door of Tolkien House was also unlocked. Above the door and surrounded by grass was a wooden board with the simple declaration: HOBBIT HOME. The overall appearance was enough to render it recognizable as "Tolkien House."

Just inside and on the left was a quaint living room with a fireplace and comfortable, mismatched chairs and sofas. A bookshelf featured multiple editions of *The Lord of the Rings* trilogy, and boxed hardcover editions of *The Hobbit* and *The Silmarillion.* Framed prints of hobbits, Gandalf the wizard, the dragon Smaug, and other lively creatures covered the walls. The rooms each had a round door, a bed, a round nightstand with a reading lamp, and a porthole window. The facilities were in the back.

Outside, Salome noted that Tolkien House was in line with the southwest point of the star. However, the grass covering the structure would protect it from the relentless energy of the poison arrow.

"A red door is very auspicious," Salome told Marcella.

"The color attracts good ch'i and opportunities. In fact, my front door is very much like this one."

Clouds began to form overhead, and a sea breeze ruffled their hair. They picked up their pace as the temperature dropped, briskly crossing the lawn, thick hedges to the left.

"Toby must have been quite a character."

"Oh, he was. If only he'd taken things more seriously."

"How do you mean?"

"He was too easygoing to really cut it as a businessman. And he loved to play computer games when he should have been working."

"What about Ivy? Did she ever work at Toys for Techies?"

"In marketing. But she wasn't really happy in the hi-tech industry. She's more into fashion."

They halted a few feet from the drive. A few cars passed, and they could clearly hear the surf pounding against the cliffs just on the other side of the highway. Rotting pumpkins were scattered here and there, the bulk sold, Marcella said, after the area was released as a crime scene. She had erected a small white cross in the place where Toby's body had been found.

"Do you, uh, feel anything?"

Salome laughed. "What I feel is that someone needs to get out here with a backhoe. Like up at the Playhouse, the rotting pumpkins would at least do some good as fertilizer."

"This is where the stand was," Marcella said. "This is the helpful people gua, right?"

"Of the patch only. On the property as a whole, this is part of the career gua."

"I like helpful people better. Toby was a helpful guy. Did lots of good things for people. Sometimes I think he was too nice and got taken advantage of."

"By his sister, maybe?"

"Her and that creepy attorney, Ross Prenderville."

"Are they living together?"

"Oh, no! She's way traditional. Kind of weird, since her parents were so eccentric. Or maybe it's because of it. She wants a big church wedding, the honeymoon, the whole bit. Not to mention marrying a *lawyer*," she said, the emphasis suggesting her dislike of the profession.

"They sleep together, but he always leaves before morning."

"He stayed this weekend."

"Yes, well, the weather and all—Ivy couldn't very well kick him out in the storm. Even she's not that cruel."

"How did they meet?"

"Through Toby. Ross was his attorney. It worried me when he started taking more and more control of the company. But that's just what Toby wanted. He wasn't all that interested in the business end of things, and he was happy to let Ross take care of the money."

"And the company failed."

"Yeah. Makes you wonder." Marcella's eyes narrowed, her attention over Salome's shoulder. "Speak of the devil."

Ross, behind the wheel of his gold Lexus, pulled up to the two women. He rolled down the window. "Hop in. We'll give you a ride up to the house."

"I'll walk," Marcella said.

Salome squeezed Marcella's arm. "We'll talk later. Thanks for the tour." Salome moved up to the car and climbed into the backseat. "How'd it go with the O'Kellys?"

"We can discuss that later." Ivy turned in her seat and called out to Marcella, "Did you take those clothes to the thrift shop like I asked?"

Marcella frowned. "Well, yes. Thursday."

Ivy smiled. "We'll be packing up some more things. Maybe you could drop them off."

"They're closed on Sunday."

"I didn't mean you had to take them today."

Ross sped up the road, further displaying his aggressive driving. Ivy glanced over her shoulder at Salome. "Marcella sometimes forgets to do what I tell her. Too many years on drugs, I suppose, affected her memory."

At the top of the hill, all three exited the Lexus. Salome walked over to her truck and collected her satchel from the front seat. Ivy unlocked the front door and pushed it open, waiting for Salome. While going up the steps, Salome noticed Prenderville strutting in front of the house, looking around like the lord of all he surveyed. She pushed him from her thoughts, concentrating on the entrance.

The steps were worn but not crumbling, the wooden porch weathered and in need of paint. Adirondack chairs were placed on either side of a mosaic-topped table for the enjoyment of the spectacular view of the deep green grass and blue sea.

Salome set her satchel on one of the chairs. "I need a moment to clear my mind before I enter. So give me a minute if you would."

"Whatever," Ivy said flatly. She disappeared inside, leaving the door ajar.

Salome couldn't recall any consultation where the client had been so unenthusiastic. But when she thought of it, she realized it was her mother and Waterhouse Properties that were the actual clients.

Salome placed her left hand lightly on her right, thumbs nearly touching, closed her eyes and took several deep breaths. As all around her began to melt away, she inwardly began to chant, *om ma ni pad mi om.* By the ninth chant, her body was relaxed, her mind open. With eyes still closed, she entered the house and quietly shut the door behind her.

At first she felt nothing. But gradually two distinct impressions began to form: to the right and up around shoulder height, she sensed aggressive, mercurial energy. Down near the floor and up to about her waist, the energy was sluggish and heavy, as if something were drawing it down.

She opened her eyes and looked around the large foyer, which was impressively paneled in mahogany. To the left and straight ahead were two sets of sliding doors, also mahogany, both sets closed. In the center of the left wall was a long table with an old aerial photograph of the institute hanging above it. Salome turned to her right, where Ivy stood on the staircase, her hand on the banister. Beyond the stairs, a corridor branched off to the right.

"My rooms are upstairs," she announced, which Salome supposed was something of a command. She collected her satchel from the porch and went up the stairs.

At the top of the carpeted staircase, Salome followed Ivy, who hurried down the hall then entered the farthest room on the right. This west-facing bedroom was full of light. The walls, furnishings, and bedding were white. Black accent rugs were scattered on the hardwood floor. The queen-sized bed was just inside the door facing the window; not a good position, as while in bed, the entrance could not be seen except peripherally. Clearly, the bed had been placed to take advantage of the compelling sea view. The room had no personal items displayed, or color, and Salome's impression was one of impermanence.

Ivy opened the door to the adjacent bathroom. She must have seen something she didn't like. "Just a minute," she said.

When Salome entered, Ivy was putting a couple of towels in a wicker hamper. The woman was neat and tidy, almost obsessively so.

The bathroom fixtures looked to be circa the 1950s, the color scheme, including the shower curtain, shades of green. They walked on through and into another bedroom, this one also stark and simply furnished with twin beds and a shared nightstand between them.

"The guest room," Ivy said.

"When was the house built?"

Ivy shrugged. "The nineteen twenties, I think. Maybe earlier. My father inherited the house from his parents. Several generations have lived here."

"Remodels?"

"My grandparents remodeled the place in the nineteen

fifties. Later, my parents were more focused on putting up the houses at the institute. They didn't bother making any changes here, but as you can see, it has been well maintained—which your parents probably want to know."

Ivy exited through the guest bedroom door and went out into the hall and down to the room opposite the white bedroom. Salome followed her inside.

This, the relationship gua, had been turned into a dressing room to accommodate Ivy's extensive wardrobe. Many racks encircled the room. A three-paneled mirror more than six feet tall blocked the south-facing window, in the room's children/creativity gua.

Ivy moved quickly into the adjoining bath, which was much like the one across the hall but for the addition of a vanity table. She retraced her steps through the dressing room, and they moved to the opposite end of the hall, entering Ivy's office/study through the room's career gua. A long, wide window overlooked the dairy. She had positioned her desk to face the window. Since she planned to move anyway, Salome didn't mention the risk she was taking by sitting with her back to the door. This position always suggested secret enemies and lack of control in one's professional activities. Salome walked across the hall to the room opposite and looked out the window. Sure enough, the harsh energy from the easternmost point of the administration building's star shot right through this part of the house.

She returned to Ivy's office.

"What's below this room?"

"Toby's office."

"Is there an attic?"

"Yes, but there's nothing up there."

"Let's have a look downstairs then."

Ivy led her along the corridor beyond the stairs, where the kitchen, the dining room, and the living room were located.

If the contents of the walk-in pantry were any indication, the quaint country kitchen was wasted on the current tenants. Stocked with cases upon cases of cream-filled cakes, macaroni and cheese, soft drinks, Halloween candy, and boxes of cereal, it was a kid's dream.

"I usually eat out," Ivy stated.

From the kitchen, they entered the dining room, located in the relationship gua of the house, same as Ivy's wardrobe room directly above. The room smelled of must, and the curtains were closed. The huge hutch, china cabinet, and the oak table and eight chairs looked more lonely than impressive. Dust furred a centerpiece of red and green Christmas balls, plastic holly, and berries.

Across the hall was the front room, or living room. On the south side was a traditional fireplace, far less obtrusive than the wedge in the Playhouse. Framed family pictures were in a box on top of a baby grand piano. There were faded couches and chairs, and bookcases in the process of being emptied.

"As you can see, I've already started boxing up things in here," Ivy said.

Leaving the family room, they returned to the foyer. "If you'd prefer, I'll have a look at Toby's rooms by myself."

"Oh, no," Ivy said, half-suggesting that Salome might pocket something.

"Shall we, then?" Salome said pleasantly.

Ivy slid back the doors just to the left of the front door, and they entered a long bedroom. Like Ivy's bed, his was positioned beside the door, to the right. They both would have been better off having their beds at an angle to the door in the command position. His bed faced two windows that looked out on the Playhouse. Some rosebushes that were in need of care grew outside his window. He had his own television in the corner directly across from the door. Had he been around, Salome would have suggested he cover the TV when it was not in use, which brought to mind the TV in the armoire in the Playhouse, which could be closed off.

On and under the nightstand was a jumble of paperback

science fiction. The ceiling was covered with a star map, like the one in the Playhouse, this one larger and more extensive.

A small bathroom was in the family/health gua. The door from the bedroom opened onto the toilet. Opposite the toilet was a tub and shower, with a window above the tiled wall.

"This is cute," Salome said, indicating the penguin-covered shower curtain.

"A promotional giveaway from some dot com with a penguin for a logo. You wouldn't believe all the stuff that's given away; lunch boxes, water bottles, toys. One company even sent telescopes as a promo tool."

Stepping around the toilet, Ivy opened the other door, and they entered Toby's office/computer room. His desk was straight ahead in the wealth position of the room and the house. Salome figured he had probably left both doors to the bathroom open and the toilet seat and lid up—very bad for finances, but hardly atypical. All around the room were tables piled with assorted computer components; cables sat in disarray underneath. Bookshelves took up most of the wall space, the library featuring computer-related literature and games. At least the desk was in the command position, facing and at an angle to the main door.

She asked Ivy if Toby had made any recent changes to his rooms.

"I wouldn't know. I never came in here."

"What about maid service?" she inquired, thinking a maid would know of changes he might have made.

"Marcella used to clean. But after Toby's death, I didn't feel comfortable having her in the house," she replied impatiently, quickly changing the subject. "So what do you think—about the house—not this mess?" Ivy crossed the room and slid back the doors to the foyer.

"It's a fine, sturdy house, no missing guas. The exterior needs painting and trees for protection, but the interior is in good condition—"

Just then Ross charged into the foyer, looking excited.

"The police are here!"

Ivy glanced at Salome then back to Ross.

"Excuse me," Ivy said and hurried out of the room.

From his position in the doorway, Ross regarded Salome for a moment. He seemed torn between leaving her alone and joining Ivy outside. Finally he said, "You can leave now, Ms. Waterhouse."

Salome picked up her satchel and followed him outside, where she stopped on the porch. A police cruiser and a late model blue sedan had pulled up at the edge of the patch of lawn in front of the Playhouse. She saw Marcella open the front door to the two police officers and Detective Child. Ivy and Ross hurried toward the house.

Curiosity got the better of her, and Salome bustled down the steps.

The front door of the Playhouse stood open, and she could hear voices as she entered, alarm growing with each step she took down the hall.

Ivy's voice could be heard above the others. ". . . I'd forgotten about it, you see and . . . oh, my God!"

Salome moved around the corner, just as Child removed what appeared to be a badly stained shop cloth or rag from a section of the fireplace wedge, clearly a well-concealed hidey-hole. He carefully unwrapped the stiff cloth, his hands gloved in supple latex, and held out a carving knife, the blade crusted with blood.

Ross's expression was grave. Marcella appeared to have been punched in the stomach. For a moment, the room fell completely silent. Then Ivy suddenly screamed and lunged at Marcella.

"You killed my brother! You murdered Toby!"

Ross grabbed Ivy and held her close.

"Did you kill Carla Whitmore, too?" Ivy cried, her face contorted in anger. "You did, didn't you? To bring disgrace on the institute—just when it was starting up again. Jealousy, all the years living in the shadow of my family! Oh, God, I wish I'd never let Toby talk me into letting you come back here!"

Detective Child read Marcella her rights. The two uniformed officers moved on either side of Marcella and handcuffed her.

Salome went back down the hall and outside. In a moment, the group, with Marcella and her police escort in the lead, exited the Playhouse. Marcella looked at Salome, all the sparkle and life gone from her eyes. "I didn't kill anyone," she said sadly, but holding herself with dignity. "I swear."

With Ivy tucked under his arm, Ross said again, "I think you'd better leave, Ms. Waterhouse."

A few moments later, Salome stood at the top of the drive watching the procession. After helping Ivy into the passenger seat of his car, Ross had gone inside and brought out Ivy's handbag, then locked the front door of the Big House. Why hadn't Marcella mentioned the hidey-hole? Salome wondered. Of course, there was one good reason. She didn't know about it. But Ivy did.

The view of the valley now suddenly seemed sinister rather than pastoral.

On the return drive to Holyrood, she wondered where Detective Child would be this evening: with Phyllis at the Beach Bistro in Holyrood village or in front of a gaggle of media at the police station?

Chapter 15

☯

PHYLLIS consulted her watch for the umpteenth time. She looked around the restaurant, at the balloons and decorations, the table with champagne and plastic champagne glasses set up by the length of glass, with a sliding door overlooking the beach. Everyone who happened to come in was welcome to partake along with the guests. Finally, with an annoyed expression on her face, Phyllis's eyes came to rest on Salome, who stood beside her at the bar.

"If he's not here in fifteen minutes, I'm calling off the engagement."

"You said that five minutes ago, Phyl," Salome noted.

"Yeah, well I *mean* it this time."

Phyllis's impatience was partly understandable. She hadn't been in love for years—the last time in her twenties, when she'd been married to Manderson "Mandy" Monroe. After a second marriage to an actress, Mandy had finally accepted his homosexuality. He'd been out of the closet for some time now, and he and Phyllis had become good friends.

"Does Mandy know about Gordon?"

"Mandy's in Paris. So, no."

"I guess his health must be okay if he's able to travel," Salome said, the comment significant, as Mandy had AIDS.

"He's hanging in there. Mandy always has been a survivor."

Barbara Boatwright moved up to the two women. After taking a sip of champagne, she said, "Gordon Child must be one helluva detective, solving *two* murders in one day."

Salome didn't have the heart to contradict, not in front of Phyllis. She considered Gordon Child to be more lucky than clever. What appeared to be the conclusion of both the Ashcroft and the Whitmore murders was the night's hot topic.

That morning, Roger Cane had been arrested at the boathouse of a physician in Sausalito. Cane had driven to his friend's residence after allegedly being attacked by Carla Whitmore in the chapel at the institute. His friend had stitched his wounds and finally convinced Cane to call the police.

According to Cane, he'd been meditating in the chapel when Carla burst in brandishing a knife. He said she'd been stalking him for months, sending hate mail, and attempting to ruin his reputation, all because she considered him an accessory to her sister's murder. He said his only crime had been to support his publisher, the husband of Carla's sister, who had been acquitted in the beating death of his wife.

They struggled and, in self-defense, he "accidentally" strangled her. Once he realized she was dead, he staunched the flow of blood from the cuts and jabs on his arms and torso then carried her body back to her room, entering through the window, which he said had been open. A key in her pocket told him where she was staying. In the room, he stripped off her clothing and dressed her in a robe he found on the bed. Because her clothes were stained with his blood, he gathered them along with the knife and took the bundle to his car. He then went back to his cubicle at Dogbert House. By then all the lights were out and no one saw him grab his things and leave.

Like many of the guests here at the Beach Bistro, Salome had seen Cane being arrested on the 6 o'clock news. Gone was the confidence and fluid body movements she'd witnessed Friday night. He looked traumatized and rigid, and Salome had instantly thought of those poison arrows aimed at both the chapel and Dogbert House. Had Cane been another victim of the lethal energy?

When Salome arrived at the party, rather than holding back, Phyllis had been excited, even anxious to relate the details of Cane's story as told to her by Gordon, information not yet released. But then, Salome had been first to point out a possible connection between Roger Cane and Carla Whitmore, which led Phyllis to uncover the details of Carla's sister's murder.

Then there was Marcella's arrest. Phyllis had confided that Ross Prenderville called Gordon, suggesting that he get a warrant to take another look at the Playhouse. Ivy, Gordon had said, had suddenly remembered the hidey-hole where she and Toby used to put their "treasures" when they were children. Ivy thought Marcella might have known about it and kept drugs there.

Footage of Marcella being taken into custody had not been timely enough to make the early news, but no doubt the story would appear on the 10 o'clock broadcast. Salome thought the drug excuse was just a bit too convenient in light of what had been found, leaving her with the impression that poor Marcella was little more than a pawn being sacrificed in a much bigger game.

When Barbara moved off, Salome said, "You know, Phyl, if he really does go into politics, he'll be married to the limelight."

"But being stood up at my own engagement party is a bit much!"

"Good practice, though, for a politician's wife. Enjoy yourself, and you'll make him proud."

"Of course, this is just an *informal* engagement party," Phyllis rationalized. She looked at her watch again. "But maybe I'll just get drunk and hit on Ralph," she said, casting around for Holyrood's best-looking surfer-cop, Ralph Blue.

Salome plucked a garlic-stuffed olive from a bowl on the bar, an indication kissing wasn't on her agenda tonight. Just as she finished one and reached for another, Phyllis brightened. "Well, there's the reason you traded in your futon."

Salome followed Phyllis's gaze. Michael O'Kelly stood just inside the restaurant, appearing surprised by the activity and decorations. Salome dropped the olive back into the bowl. Her nerves suddenly came to life. Her heart picked up the pace, and she couldn't seem to catch her breath. Then she spun around and stared into the mirror behind the bar. Michael started for the bar. She looked around for something to mask the taste of garlic and grabbed a piece of bread. She ducked her head and chewed.

"Phyllis. Nice to see you. What's going on?"

"Things were getting too quiet around here. We decided to have a party. Help yourself to champagne, Michael."

Phyllis poked Salome in the ribs then moved off.

"Salome?"

Salome swallowed the lump of bread, which went down like a jagged stone. She turned and smiled. For a middle-aged man, you couldn't do much better in the pulchritude department. Last time she'd seen him, he'd been carrying the burden of family and business problems, a combination that dropped weight from his body and added wear to his face. Now though, he appeared to be in fine shape, his handsome features possessed of an underlying strength. Even the gray hair suited his looks. It happened; some people just looked better after enduring a crisis or two.

"Michael. How're you doing?" Was it possible his eyes had actually gotten bluer?

"Fine. So what *is* going on?"

"An engagement party. An *informal* engagement party.

"Ah. Anyone I know?"

His eyes nailed her, puncturing a place of stored emotion. The feelings began oozing out, each one more intense than the last. She quickly glanced away.

"Phyl."

"My, my. Well, that calls for a drink." He motioned to the bartender. "What are you having, Salome?"

"A beer would be nice. Thanks."

When his scotch rocks and her domestic beer arrived, he raised his glass. "Cheers. Good to see you."

"And you."

"I don't see anyone attached to Phyl. Where's the lucky guy?"

"Hasn't arrived yet."

"Who is he?"

"You probably don't know him. He's a homicide detective. His name is Gordon Child."

"Of course I know him! Or rather know *of* him. Jesus, Salome, you think I just crawled out from under a rock?"

Salome started. "Sorry, Michael. I forget you live here now."

"And own the paper."

"I thought your mother—"

"Mother has Alzheimer's. She's in a home in Monterey."

"Oh, Michael, I'm so sorry."

"Anyway, I've taken over various family businesses." Then he added pointedly, "Including Uncle Francis's realty company."

"The realty company," Salome said slowly. Her initial reaction to seeing him transmogrified into something unpleasant.

He gave her a hard look, one all too familiar. A look the O'Kellys reserved for the Waterhouses. But it appeared for just an instant and then was gone.

Salome drank some of her beer.

"We're interested in the Ashcroft property." The challenge in his tone was unmistakable.

"Well, good luck."

"I know your father's bidding on it."

Should she tell him why? That her father would just love to see O'Kelly Realty go bankrupt. No, she wouldn't tell him. He was being a jerk, living up to the family name. But it reminded her she needed to talk to her parents about the property—very soon.

A tall blonde who was probably in her late twenties or early thirties, wearing a black cocktail dress and carrying a beaded bag, walked up and placed a kiss on Michael's cheek.

"Sorry I'm late."

"Meg Stanley, Salome Waterhouse."

The two women exchanged tepid hellos.

"Meg's an investment banker, visiting from Boston."

"Ah, your old profession," Salome remarked and put her bottle on the bar.

"My firm sent me out here to talk Michael into coming back."

"Now why'd you have to go and say that? I thought it was my blue eyes."

"If you're having dinner here, I recommend the cioppino," Salome said, trying to make a pleasant exit. "Thanks for the drink, Michael. And good luck with the Ashcroft deal. I mean that."

"Good seeing you, Salome."

Taking care with each step, refraining from sprinting, Salome walked toward the door. Phyllis stepped in front of her.

"Don't you hate old boyfriends who flaunt younger women?" Phyllis said, looking sincerely angry and a little drunk.

"So what's the status? Ralph or Gordon?"

Phyllis smiled. "It was close there for a minute. Just talked to my knight errant. He's on his way. I tell you, though, Ralph looked damn good. Still does. Just so you know, the formal engagement party will be this coming Friday night at the Fairmont Hotel in San Jose. Gordon's taking care of that one, which means there'll be a lot of potential contributors."

She leaned in close and said in a low tone, "If you leave now, he'll think it's because you can't bear the sight of him with a babe. He'll gloat. Nothing worse than a gloating man. Stay. Get drunk with me then go home and rip the tag off the new mattress!"

Salome laughed, feeling a bit better but finding it strange that Phyl would be the one to lift her spirits.

Ralph Blue appeared. "How ya doin', Salome?" His sun-streaked hair was past regulation length, but he received no complaints from his boss. A well-respected champion surfer, Ralph kept a lot of young kids away from drugs and related criminal activity. Haircuts were not an issue where Ralph was concerned.

"I'm fine, Ralph."

"Can I get you something? Champagne? A mixed drink?"

"A beer. Yeah, I'd like a beer."

As soon as Ralph moved away, Salome said to Phyllis, "Did you tell him to do that?"

"Of course not. Ralph's always had a thing for you."

At that moment Gordon arrived and the ch'i in the restaurant rose considerably. With Phyllis at his side, he smiled broadly, tirelessly shaking hands and making small talk. He regarded Salome as if they were meeting for the first time, as if he'd forgotten the interview.

Once their brief encounter concluded, she joined her parents. Reggie was just saying to Satomi, "I guess you were right, honey. It is love this time."

"How can you tell, Dad?"

"He showed up."

"About the Ashcroft property," Salome began. She went on to describe the various houses, concluding with the administration building and its dominant and "very bad ch'i, which affects the entire area." She paused to take a drink of her beer.

"So I recommend that you drop the deal unless you

want to do something about the administration building. But removal of the seven projectiles would be costly, as they're part of the roof, which of course would need to be replaced."

"Your recommendation wouldn't have anything to do with Michael O'Kelly's involvement with his family's realty company?" her father asked.

"No, Dad," she said, subduing a flame of ire. "This is strictly a professional assessment."

SOME TIME LATER, SALOME STOOD IN HER bedroom regarding the new decorating scheme with a critical eye. She'd walked home from the Beach Bistro a few minutes after Michael and Meg departed. She'd seen Michael stop and look around just before leaving and flattered herself with the thought that he'd been looking for her.

After a couple minutes, she put her beer down, one she'd opened in the kitchen and her favorite brand, Kirin. She walked over to the painting of the couple strolling on the beach. They looked as bland as the sand, the scene as hokey and insipid as Elvis on velvet.

"What was I thinking, ShiShi?"

ShiShi kept his thoughts to himself but did do his feline best to supervise.

After propping the painting to one side of the front door, Salome stripped the bed. The neatly folded sheets, duvet, and pink satin bedspread joined the seascape couple.

She plucked a fresh Kirin from the refrigerator and returned to the bedroom.

What she lacked in body strength she more than made up for in determination and patience. It took an hour, even with ShiShi supervising, but finally she managed to reduce the bed to its components and move them out of the bedroom and into and around the foyer. It was clutter, but neat clutter, and would not be at the entrance of her house long enough to make a difference.

In the utility room she collected the rolled matting, individual tatami mats attached by duct tape, and hauled it back to the bedroom. Adding the single rug to the pile in the foyer, she unrolled the matting, once again enjoying the fresh, grassy scent.

She carried the lightweight *tokatsu*, a cabinet topped with a niche, from her walk-in closet back to its original position, where the bed had been, in the relationship gua. From the bottom cabinet, she pulled out her trusty futon and rolled it out on the floor. The narrow bedding had not seen action other than sleep, but she'd also never had back problems while using it.

From a smaller cabinet above the one that housed the futon, she removed a brass incense burner fashioned like an androgynous Buddha, matches, and a stick of *hoyeh-koh*, Eternal Treasure, incense. Returning her old familiar things to their original positions was comforting and dispersed some of the disappointment created by her illusions. The other items were too alien for this house. At the same time, maybe she was just overreacting to seeing Michael with another woman, the beer loosening her emotions.

She sat cross-legged on the futon, her back to the wall, and the *tokatsu* to her right. The one item that had not been moved, which Phyllis suggested should be, was the delicately detailed image of Kwan Yin on white silk, her sky-crown azure blue. The first sight on waking, the last seen before sleep, the Chinese goddess of mercy and compassion seemed to exemplify Salome's purpose in Holyrood-by-the-Sea.

She'd come back to be close to her aging parents, to help them whenever and wherever needed.

Salome stared at the benevolent face of the goddess. The opalescent eyes regarded her above the urn out of which water poured in an eternal stream.

Giving was her raison d'être in Holyrood, and that was

a good thing. She had to be careful of wanting something in return, especially if that something involved Michael O'Kelly.

Finally, turning out the small lamp, and with ShiShi curled at the bottom of the futon, she stretched out, her thoughts again on giving. Closing her eyes, she decided on an action that could easily toss her life into the spin cycle.

Chapter 16

SALOME pulled back the living room curtains, unlocked and slid the door open, and stepped out onto the patio. She breathed deeply of the fresh morning air and stepped out onto the thick grass. Waves from the bay softly lapped against the cliffs. Off to the left, she could hear the burbling pond in the Japanese garden just off the kitchen. Overhead, lavender streaks and gold splotches were mixed as if with an impasto knife. She welcomed the lovely morning but decided that a change of venue might be in order to activate her mind; at the moment her home seemed just a little too restful.

She made coffee, dressed in warm clothes, and grabbed a pen and a notebook. Once behind the wheel of her pickup, she drove to the other side of the village to the overlook.

The automobiles—trucks, vans, and sedans alike—were, for the most part, old and indistinguishable. This was where those who lived inland came to claim a few moments of peace. But people with expensive cars had enough toys or great views to occupy them and wouldn't bother with the grits and gravy semisolitude the lookout provided.

Salome pulled into a space between a Dodge Dart and a VW sporting a surfboard. She poured coffee out of a thermos and looked out, her eyes moving from the sandy arc of Holyrood Beach, to the small restaurants and shops behind the sea wall, to the scattered storybook cottages nestled among trees and shrubs, and finally resting on the church on Holyrood Hill, which, from this distance, didn't look quite so much like the old pile it was.

Off to the left, but at the moment blocked by the Dodge Dart with a teenage driver wearing a reverse-facing baseball cap and scribbling in a notebook propped on the steering wheel, was the Perfume Mansion. But she wasn't that interested in looking at her property this morning.

She sipped the hot brew, her attention shifting to the long wooden finger of the pier that seemed to point to a pod of surfers bobbing on the calm water, diehards waiting for a wave.

After a while, the muzzy clouds from last night's beer began to move off, leaving enough clear patches to order her thoughts. She picked up the notebook and pen. Then, like the young driver in the rusting Dodge Dart, who was probably doing homework, she began scribbling notes.

When the thermos was empty, she drove home. In the study, she turned on the gas wall heater and put a tape of a string quartet in the boom box. She sat behind the desk and went over the notes she'd made.

At 8 o'clock she telephoned Marybeth Stoops.

"Salome! My goodness. Long time, no see. Not in any trouble, are you?"

Salome laughed. "No, but a friend is."

"Well, come on over. I'm free until ten."

"Great! Give me fifteen minutes."

When they rang off, Salome called a friend who ran several social service programs in Santa Cruz and arranged for the bed to be picked up that afternoon.

*　　*　　*

MARYBETH STOOPS WAS A SEMIRETIRED AT-
torney who lived in a small cottage squeezed between two
mammoth new houses on the Bluff, the informal designation of this section of Holyrood, and just a block west
of Salome. She'd been offered a fortune for the property
but steadfastly refused to sell. The house had been in her
family since the 1920s. Born and bred in San Francisco,
Marybeth had spent many a summer vacation within its
walls and knew that whomever bought the house would
immediately tear it down. She couldn't bear the thought
of the sturdy little structure, its walls permeated with so
many happy memories, being swept away and replaced
by some soulless beacon to wealth and ostentation. She
also knew that the two redwoods in the back would likely
be cut down, the wood sold. She was one of a breed who
couldn't be extracted from her place by any amount of
money.

Across the front of the white one-story house was a
long porch with an overhang supported by four narrow
beams painted yellow. A healthy jade plant flourished in
a terra cotta pot by the front door, the rounded succulent
leaves symbolic of coins and hence money. And being by
the front door, the energy of the plant would attract prosperity into the house.

Marybeth must have seen her coming. She pulled open
the door just as Salome's hand was poised to knock.

"Gosh! It's so good to see you, Salome!"

The two women hugged, Marybeth, being nearly six
feet tall, having to bend down. Her hair was a thick pro-
fusion of salt and pepper curls. She wore a starched white
linen shirt, with a black velvet scarf hanging down the
front and a pair of black slacks and black pumps.

She pulled back and regarded Salome with kind gray
eyes with deep laugh lines extending to the hairline. She
had a hearty, robust spirit that enabled her to find the
amusing elements in the human condition. Being a criminal defense attorney, this aspect of her character had

spared her from the many negatives associated with dealing with tragedy and crime on a regular basis.

Widowed young, she had never remarried. Occasionally, the two women would bump into each other at one of the local restaurants. Marybeth always seemed to be accompanied by much younger men. Breast cancer had initially reduced her workload five years ago, but she was gradually picking up her former pace. That Marybeth agreed to see Salome told her she might have time to take care of Salome's legal needs. But would she be willing?

"Want some coffee? Or would you prefer tea? Got all kinds."

"Coffee's fine," Salome said and followed Marybeth into her comfortable, airy office just to the right of the door in, appropriately, the helpful people gua—a position well-suited to Marybeth's inclinations and character.

When the two women settled in comfortable chairs facing the window with mugs of freshly brewed French roast, Marybeth with a legal pad propped on her lap, Salome told the attorney about Marcella Cruz's arrest then backed up and talked about her recent experiences at the Star Institute. Marybeth said she was familiar with the Ashcroft murder case, so Salome only added information she'd gleaned over the past few days, particularly Marcella's relationship with Toby Ashcroft.

"I want to post bail for Marcella."

"You don't consider her a flight risk?"

"Like I said, I believe she's innocent."

"Not the same thing, Salome. Innocent or guilty she could flee."

After a moment, Salome answered. "She won't flee. Not if she's remanded into my custody."

Marybeth raised her eyebrows but instead of commenting, she took a deep breath and said, "This could take a couple of weeks, Salome."

"That won't do. I want her out and in my custody ASAP. I think jail will be extremely detrimental to her health—mentally and physically."

"Finding a judge to expedite a bail hearing won't be

easy. Even in Santa Cruz, they've got full dockets. Besides, it'll be even harder if the arresting officer is well respected around the court."

Salome hadn't thought about that. Certainly plans for a political future indicated someone who believed strongly in his own reputation.

"You have to try. I know in my heart she's innocent."

"Offhand I can't think of any judge who'd grant bail just on the strength of your belief in the young woman's character."

"Look, she's Indian. Ohlone."

"Is she an activist?"

"She's just an ordinary person caught up in a bad situation. Do you know any Native American judges? Or judges sympathetic to Indians?"

Instead of answering, Marybeth asked a question, upsetting but not unusual. "Any drinking or drug problems?"

"Hey, just because she's Indian doesn't mean she's automatically a druggie or an alcoholic."

"Unfortunately, the stereotype exists, Salome, so deal with it. Does she have a drug or drinking problem?"

Salome swallowed hard, her mouth dry. She sipped her coffee. "In the past. But she's open about it, mentioned it to me freely. I didn't ask her."

For a long while they sat in silence. Salome hoped she wasn't in any way exacerbating Marcella's situation by involving herself.

Finally, Marybeth spoke. "I do know a judge who collects Native American art."

Salome straightened. "Great!"

"It's a start, not a promise. Let's say I can get a bail hearing. Would you appear?"

"I'd rather stay in the background." Salome mentioned Phyl's involvement with Detective Child. "Not that it would ruin their relationship, but if the cousin of his fiancée is seen supporting his prime suspect, that's just the sort of thing the press would love to milk. "But if it's necessary, I'll do it."

"You'll need to go to the courthouse to post bail."

"Right." She thought for a moment. "What if I give you the money? Really, Marybeth, I don't want to complicate things. Just get her out as quickly and quietly as possible."

"You're not going to be able to keep it secret. If you can't take the disruptions, then I'd advise against it."

Salome took a deep breath and glanced outside at the bay and faintly outlined hills beyond. She'd never had children and wondered if she might be reacting to some echo of the biological clock.

"Is there something else going on you're not telling me?"

"Let's just say I'm interested in proving Marcella's innocence and leave it at that."

Marybeth placed the yellow pad on the coffee table but kept the pen in her hand.

"I'd be remiss if I didn't say this—you're taking a great risk here, emotionally and certainly financially, especially if this goes to trial. You sure you don't want to just leave her in the care of a court-appointed attorney?"

"Absolutely not."

They discussed Marybeth's fees, then the two women looked at each other for a moment. Salome pulled out her checkbook. Marybeth handed over the pen.

BACK BEHIND THE DESK IN HER STUDY, SA-lome crossed off the first items on the list she'd compiled at the overlook—including the names of lawyers she knew in the area.

Then she regarded the single name under "Computer Nerd." After a moment, she picked up the phone and punched in the familiar number preceded by the 703 area code.

A woman answered. "Hallooo!" she sang out.

"Hi, Elle. This is Salome. Is Gabe around?"

The voice lost some enthusiasm. "Is this important?"

"Would I be calling otherwise?"

"Hold on."

The wives of ex-husbands could be so annoying. Of course, she reasoned, the reverse was also true.

She pictured Elle, an attractive, fortyish blonde, flouncing into Gabe's upstairs study (where he refused to have a phone), coming up to the writer, and stopping. With one hip jutting out in a stance of disapproval, she would extend the portable phone at arm's length, as if holding out a cockroach or dead mouse for his inspection.

He might look at her inquiringly, eyes slightly unfocused, still in his fictional world.

"It's *her*," Elle would say.

Which is exactly what Salome heard, followed by, "Salome?"

"Hi, Gabe. Sorry to bother you, but—" then she posed her question.

During the twenty years they were married, Salome had worked as his researcher. But he took care of anything related to computers, and so her knowledge of them was limited primarily to word processing. By the time she discovered the Internet, she and Gabe were divorcing and he'd hired someone else.

"Good grief, Salome. Do you know what you're asking here?"

"Of course. I want you to check out someone's financial records. You've got all the software. You know how."

He laughed. "Salome. Sometimes you are so naive. You're asking me to *hack* into someone's personal files! Christ, you think I'm nuts? We're talking *illegal*, Salome."

"Okay. Give me an idea where to start."

He laughed again. "That's like walking into an operating room and saying to the surgeon, Hey, I want to learn brain surgery, and expecting the doc to simply hand over a scalpel."

During the momentary silence, Salome imagined him sitting back in his chair, shaking his head, then sitting forward, his interest piqued.

"What's this about, anyway? Don't tell me you're writing a mystery."

She let a shrug pass through the line.

"Okay. I'll tell you where to start. Right there in Silicon Valley. Hacker central. What's the story about?"

She hadn't anticipated that question and mentally scrambled for a quick response. "I'm working it out. You know how that goes."

"Are you in some kind of financial trouble?"

In the background she heard Elle say, loud and clear, "If she wants money, no way. Hang up!"

"Of course not. Just tell me what you'd do if you needed information about a bad guy's business deals. Information that's probably very well hidden."

"I'd talk to people he works with. Find out his love interests. Or hire a P.I. You know how to research, Mei. Call an expert."

"That's what I'm doing."

"Revert to the old ways—digging through public records—tedious and boring. Or breaking and entering—quick and dramatic."

"Well, thanks for your time. Maybe I just needed to talk it out."

"When you finish, send me the manuscript. If it's any good, I'll pass it along to Don," he concluded, "Don" being his agent.

"Thanks, Gabe."

When they rang off, she turned on her computer. The conversation did bring up an idea, one she'd not thought about until Gabe mentioned Silicon Valley. Sometimes the answers right in front of you were the easiest to overlook. Just because Toys for Techies was out of business didn't mean information about the company wasn't available.

Once connected to the Internet, she typed in Toys for Techies. In moments a website appeared on the screen. There was no menu, just a message saying that the site was temporarily unavailable. However, there was an E-mail address.

Feeling a frisson of excitement, her fingers poised on the keyboard, she stared straight ahead, across the room and out the door into the foyer. After a few minutes she typed a message that included her phone number. Then she sent the mail.

Next, she looked for information on Ross Prenderville. On the Google search engine, she found several entries. The first was the website for a law firm in San Jose. Prenderville's name was included in a list of about thirty. She pointed the cursor at his name and clicked. His page appeared, devoid of any information, except that he was on a leave of absence.

Returning to the law firm's home page, she found their phone number and called. She explained to the receptionist that she was writing an article for the *Holyrood Echo* about attorneys living in Santa Cruz County, including one Ross Prenderville, but had seen on the website that he was on a leave of absence and just wanted to verify his employment with the San Jose firm.

"Actually, he left two years ago. That site needs to be updated, and his name taken off. Sorry about that. These things get overlooked."

"How long was he with your firm?"

"About a year, I think. Hold on a minute, I'll check."

Salome didn't have long to wait. When the woman came back, she said, "Let me call you back. What's the number there?"

"Actually, I'm a freelancer working at home," Salome said quickly and gave her phone number.

"My name's Melinda Brown. Let me call you on my break in about ten minutes. Is that okay?"

"No problem, Melinda. And thanks."

"Sure."

Melinda sounded eager, and Salome had the feeling she wanted something from *her*.

While waiting, and relieved she hadn't blown it, Salome looked through the remaining entries on the Google site: his inclusion on the roster of a rugby team, a mention as one of a team of lawyers trying a copyright infringement case in Silicon Valley, and finally several listings of his performances in the musical programs during the annual Highland games in Bonnie Doon over the past couple of years.

The latter gave her an idea. Still on Google, she typed in "Incredible String Band," and after some searching found the lyrics for "October Song" by Robin Williamson. While Toby Ashcroft's favorite song printed out, the phone rang.

"You understand this is kind of personal," Melinda began after they exchanged greetings. The eagerness Salome heard earlier had expanded. "We were both into music. I'm a singer, you see, on the lines of Loreena McKennitt. Anyway, he was going to help me with my career. Then, when he took leave, I stopped hearing from him. You wouldn't happen to have his number, would you?"

"Sorry, he's unlisted."

"Yeah, I know. Darn."

"What was he like?"

"Pretty refreshing, considering most of the attorneys here are gung ho Stanford grads. Being from back east, he didn't fit in easily, but I got the feeling he didn't care, that the firm was just a place to roost until something better came along. Then he took leave, and I stopped hearing from him. I did see him at the Highland Games in September. We both performed, so he couldn't avoid me, but he wasn't friendly either. When I tried to talk to him, he just said he'd call me. Didn't even introduce me to his girlfriend. I thought maybe she was the jealous type, but still, our relationship never went beyond a shared interest in music. I'm not a real beauty, but boy can I sing," she said and laughed.

"Like I said, he did say he'd help me with my singing career. If I could get his number and just talk to him one-on-one, at least I'd know if he was really serious. He said he'd look into recording contracts, that sort of thing. I don't want to bug him, but at the same time, I would like to get going with this. He said I had the potential to be a real success. I figured he wouldn't have said it if he didn't think there was money in it for both of us."

"Have you checked with the rugby club he belongs to?"

"No. I didn't know about that."

Salome gave Melinda the name of the club, and after wishing her good luck, she rang off. From the sound of it, Ross Prenderville had been looking for a source of big money as soon as he'd arrived in Silicon Valley. He may have truly been interested in promoting Melinda Brown's career but dropped the idea when something much bigger—Toys for Techies—came along.

Just a moment after she hung up, the phone rang again.

Whenever she deemed it wise to use a fictitious name—not uncommon while researching for Gabe, especially when dealing with the underworld, as she sometimes had done—she used the name of her maternal grandmother.

She picked up the receiver. "Hello?"

"Mijo Koyama?"

"Yes?"

"I'm calling in regard to your E-mail to Toys for Techies."

"Ah yes! You are—or were—one of the principles?"

"That's right, Dicken Fowler. And you're interested in investing in the company?"

"Rather than discuss this on the phone, would you be willing to meet?"

"Before we waste each other's time, you do know we're no longer in business?"

"Oh yes. But since you still have a web page, that seemed to indicate there was some hope of restarting the business."

"This is a serious inquiry?"

In the background Salome heard street noise and figured the call was being made from a cell phone, or even a pay phone. But you never knew with techies, could be a sound track Dicken Fowler played while making calls from home.

"I'm quite serious."

"Your area code tells me you're in the area."

"Santa Cruz County."

"You know Fry's Electronics on Hamilton Avenue?"

They agreed to meet for lunch at a restaurant just west of the popular electronics outlet with its funky Egyptian interior design scheme.

After leaving a message on Marybeth's machine just to tell her she'd be in San Jose in the early afternoon and providing Marybeth with the cell phone number for the second time that morning, Salome hurried into her dressing room, excited about the upcoming meeting, though she didn't have a clue what to wear with the red scarf she'd told Dicken she'd be wearing, or for that matter, what she would say to him over lunch.

Chapter 17

THE family style restaurant was crowded, and half a dozen people waited in front of her at the hostess station. A vibrant red silk scarf shot through with gold thread hung down the front of her black cashmere sweater. Black slacks and slip-ons completed the ensemble. She hadn't been inside twenty seconds, when a young man wearing a faded green, plaid flannel shirt over a Toys for Techies T-shirt and jeans with holes in the knees approached.

"Mijo Koyama?"

"You're Dicken?"

"Call me Gnome. With a 'g'."

He looked no more than about sixteen, but then, everyone under forty did these days. They shook hands, and she followed him to the last booth in the restaurant's wealth gua, where two others sat waiting. They were all dressed pretty much the same, only the colors of their shirts varying.

Gnome introduced Salome to "Monk," a small guy with thick red hair and round wire-rimmed glasses, who sat in the far left corner facing the restaurant. Monk's much larger companion, introduced as Wizard, regarded her with a cocky grin and was the best looking of the motley trio. He had thoughtful brown eyes, with a distinct Asian cast, and black hair. She thought he was probably Chinese rather than Japanese or Korean.

"Are you a cop?" Wizard asked before her bottom even touched the red cushion.

"No!"

"Are you with the IRS?" Monk asked, leaning forward.

"No."

Several more acronyms followed including the FBI and CIA.

Finally, Gnome piped in with, "Do you work for Microsoft?"

"No again."

"How about a vulture—excuse me—*venture* capitalist?" Gnome added.

Salome shook her head and sighed. The waitress finally appeared, and she ordered coffee, while the other three ordered soft drink refills.

"No one's eating?" she asked.

"We didn't want to order until we knew you actually had some money," the Wizard said, his cocky smile back in place.

"I see. Well, have whatever you want."

"Thing is, we couldn't find you anywhere," Monk said, meaning they'd been looking for information about her in cyberspace. "Which we find troubling."

Wizard squinted at her. "So, Mijo or Ms. Koyama, who are you?"

Salome took a deep breath. "A friend of Marcella Cruz."

They all looked at each other with open mouths. Gnome groaned. "Then you *don't* have any money." He shook his head. "Are you her lawyer?"

"No, I'm not her lawyer. So you know about her arrest?"

"Sure. Christ. Who woulda thought," Monk said. "She was really a nice person. Never can tell with women, I guess."

"The reason I'm here is I'd like to find out who really did kill Toby Ashcroft and—" She stopped when the waitress appeared with their drinks.

Before she could resume after the waitress left, Monk interjected, "Can you guess which one of us is the real Dicken Fowler?"

Gnome piped in, "Remember, his voice was disguised when he called."

Salome sat back thinking she'd made a big mistake, that this really was a waste of time. Still, maybe when they finished playing their games she might get something out of them. She reminded herself to be patient and looked at each one.

Though the smallest of the group and hemmed in by his larger seatmate, she decided Monk was Dicken Fowler. He had a full view of the restaurant. Someone in a leadership position would instinctively not sit with his back to the door. Wizard, while having more of a physical presence and more mobility, would also be free to fetch things. Gnome, sitting like Salome, with his back to the room, wasn't even a consideration.

"Monk," she said.

"Wrong!" Gnome said, making a sound like a blaring gong on a quiz show.

"Come on, Blaine, enough fooling around," Monk said and extended his hand across the table. "I'm Dicken, Ms. Koyama." He nodded toward Wizard. "And this is Matthew."

Salome hoped the game playing had ended and didn't bother to tell them her real name.

They talked for a while about the demise of Toys for Techies.

"After the disappointment, there was this general attitude of easy come, easy go," Dicken explained. "Thing is, we're young, and our next million is just around the corner."

Matthew said, "We all got jobs with other firms."

In their defense, Gnome, who she couldn't quite think

of as a Blaine, added, "You have to understand. We're engineers, not businesspeople."

"What about Ross Prenderville?"

"What about him?" Matthew/Wizard said, his eyes narrowing.

"Do you think he might have had anything to do with the company's failure?"

"Hey, blame lands right in Toby's lap," Gnome said. "He wasn't paying attention."

"Attention to what? Or to whom? Prenderville?"

All were reluctant to talk.

Finally, Salome came to her precise reason for contacting them. "Now, I don't want to get anyone in trouble, but would one of you be interested in taking a closer look at the business files?"

All eyes fell on Salome. Dicken said in a low voice, "You want someone to hack into Prenderville's files, right?"

Matthew threw up his hands. "Hey, I'm outta here." He dug in his back pocket, pulled out a worn trifold wallet, and tossed a ten on the table. "Nice to meet you, Ms. Koyama." He stood up. "Later, guys."

Gnome checked his watch. "I've got a meeting at three." In a moment, he too was gone, leaving behind another ten and the distinct smell of fear.

"This isn't Tokyo. That's a lot for a soda," Salome observed.

"We did eat. We all arrived shortly after I talked to you."

"I get the distinct feeling there's some bad feelings connected to Ross Prenderville."

"Yeah, well, he's threatened us all with major lawsuits. *Major*. We'd all just as soon he didn't even know we're still alive. When you sent that E-mail, we wondered if maybe you were fronting for Prenderville. Plain old curiosity—and hope that you might actually be serious—determined that we'd take the meeting. All of us would love to see TFT back in business."

"Has anyone even tried to"—she paused—"investigate Prenderville?" It seemed best to avoid the word "hack."

"Toby."

"Really?" she said in surprise.

"And look what happened to him."

"How do you know? Did Toby tell you?"

"Not in so many words. Blaine was right when he said Toby wasn't paying attention—hell, we were all having too much fun. But one day he, Toby that is, found something. I don't know what exactly. It might have been a questionable invoice. He asked me about a diamond, if I'd bought one and charged it to TFT. Of course, I hadn't."

"Ivy Ashcroft wears a rather impressive diamond."

"Well, I never saw it."

"When was the last time you saw her?"

"June, the last day at the TFT offices, when Blaine, Matthew, and I packed up our gear. The guard checked our boxes to make sure we weren't stealing anything then escorted each of us to our cars. She entered the building just as I was being led out. I told her I thought it was pretty rude that she hadn't even bothered to say good-bye to us."

His face reddened, matching his hair color in intensity. Around his glass, his knuckles were white. "Pisses me off every time I think about it. She acted like it was all my fault this was happening. Then Ross suddenly swooped down. Told me to get the hell off the premises, that he'd have me arrested for harassing Ivy. Not a good day at all."

"And Toby? When was the last time you saw him?"

"Not that day. He didn't show up. Gosh, I really can't remember. What I do remember, though, is the next day we each got E-mail messages that TFT was thinking of suing us for ten million dollars each. That we'd be wise to keep our mouths shut and not talk to the press or anyone about TFT and what had been going on in the company."

"That suggests something *had* been going on."

"None of us knew anything. The only person who might have known about something fishy was Toby."

"And the person who sent the E-mail."

"Right. Ross Prenderville. Look, if he is responsible, I'd like to see him hang."

"Then how about helping knot the noose?"

"I'll have to think about this."

"Just remember while you're out here in the world thinking about it, Marcella Cruz is in jail."

The waitress appeared, asking if they wanted anything else. Dicken ordered another soda. Salome shook her head.

Dicken wouldn't commit more than to say he'd "keep in touch" and handed her a business card. Salome left him sitting there staring out the window.

Driving back over the Santa Cruz Mountains to Holyrood, she was flummoxed by the attitudes of the three former principles of Toys for Techies, or TFT, as they were inclined to call it. What happened to courage, integrity—hell, even a good old-fashioned desire for revenge? Did such traits skip generations? Maybe she wasn't being fair to Dicken, Blaine, and Matthew. After all, they were young and couldn't be blamed for survivalist instincts. What did she know? She'd never lost millions before reaching the age of twenty-five, thirty.

She stopped at the grocery store and bought a supply of soda, Twinkies, HoHos, items that might be comfort foods for Marcella; and, for herself, some miso, tofu, and Kirin beer.

Even before unloading her purchases, she parked the truck just outside the front door and ran in to check the answering machine. But no one had called.

While driving the truck into the detached single-car garage, she had the distinct feeling that she might be in for some disappointments. Still, above all, Salome Waterhouse was an optimist, skewed maybe, but she could usually squeeze something positive from even the most adverse situation.

Time abruptly slowed, bumping along as if on four flats, and just when she really wanted a pick up in speed. Marybeth did not call, but then she couldn't be expected to provide hourly updates. The attorney would let Salome know when something happened and not before, leading Salome to believe she'd not found a sympathetic judge. At the same time, Marybeth had other cases.

Nor did Dicken telephone to excitedly declare he had successfully hacked into Ross Prenderville's files and found evidence of impropriety.

She rang Judah Freeman, who had the necessary and legal computer connections, leaving a message on his machine requesting a background check on Ross Prenderville. She also mailed him a check for his time.

She went through the house and reinforced each helpful people gua by ringing a bell, chanting, and verbalizing her need.

Tuesday night Judah called to say that Ross Prenderville had never been arrested—not even for speeding, which she considered lucky—and had an excellent credit rating. And since they'd last talked, nothing new had developed regarding Duncan Mah.

On Wednesday, she dissected the lyrics of "October Song," looking for clues, certainly a long shot that left her feeling rather foolish.

But finally, on Thursday, everything changed. Time's vehicle got four new tires and a brand-new, fuel-injected engine.

Chapter 18

☯

"NOT gay, are you?"

"No, Marcella, I'm not gay. And even if I were, I doubt if I'd write such a large check for your company. Even my good nature has limits."

It was 8:30 A.M. on Thursday morning, and Marcella sat in the passenger seat of her truck while Salome drove on Highway 1 back to Holyrood. Marybeth had succeeded in getting a bail hearing that lasted all of five minutes. Salome had managed to post bail in the county clerk's office and whisk Marcella out of the courthouse before anyone who might be interested managed to pick the sleep out of their eyes.

Salome glanced over at Marcella, slumped in the passenger seat, wearing the same clothes she'd been arrested in, including that coat Salome had come to dislike intensely. Rather than shielding her from the cold, it seemed to burden her with an unfair declaration of social inferiority.

The morning was overcast, Mother Nature waiting to decide how to work this particular situation: do we flood or do we sprinkle? The light moisture made the road slick, and Salome focused on driving, mainly on what other drivers were doing.

After a while she said, "You okay?"

Marcella opened her eyes. "It's weird. About the only place us Indians—excuse me, *Native Americans*—" she said in a plumy mocking voice indicative of her disdain, "are respected is in jail. By the inmates, anyway. So yes, I'm fine. I was treated like a queen."

Salome concentrated on driving.

"So why did you bail me out?"

Salome switched on her left-turn indicator and moved out from behind an SUV, where the faces of children were muted behind windows smeared with handprints.

"Something in my nature balks when I see the wrong person incarcerated."

Salome passed the SUV.

"You don't think all the years of being in the *shadow* of the Ashcrofts made me slit Toby's throat?"

"Nope." Salome explained that she'd spent twenty years working as a researcher for best-selling author Gabriel Hoya, and in doing so had developed a sense for the good guys and the bad guys.

Marcella regarded Salome with a bit more respect. "Wow. And I thought you were just a nice feng shui lady."

"Isn't there a real bed around?" Marcella asked, after Salome showed her around the cottage and told her the one rule: shoes were not worn in the house.

"If you'd like, I can put you up at Otter Haven."

"You're joking?"

"Of course not."

"I mean, that's like the best place to stay on the coast outside Carmel."

"Would you like to stay there?"

Marcella shook her head. "This isn't fair. Of course I'd love to stay there. That's where—"

"What?"

Marcella sighed, pursed her lips, and looked down at the floor then up at the ceiling. "That's where Toby wanted to go for our honeymoon. One of the storybook cottages."

"Marcella, my parents own Otter Haven. If you want a cottage, I'll get you a cottage."

Marcella burst into tears. After a few minutes, Salome said, "Come on, let's go see my mother." She grabbed her purse, intending to pay for the cottage with a credit card.

Flight risk pulsated in banner headlines, but Marcella's absolute joy while looking around cottage 3 with its sea view negated the warning. What the hell, Salome thought, even it she splits, the pleasure of seeing her happy overpowered logical considerations.

Satomi handed over the key. "Anything you need, dear, we have staff on call twenty-four hours a day. Just pick up the phone." Satomi left.

Salome stood by the door and said, "In the meantime, no one will bother you. Only my mother and I know where you are."

Marcella threw her arms around Salome's neck. Withdrawing from the clutch, Salome said, "Come over whenever you want. We can have lunch, dinner, whatever."

"After a shower, I think I'll just take it easy. Maybe catch a bite in the lodge. You've all ready done enough for me."

Outside, the clouds had drifted to the east, opening up the sky to bright sunshine. Feeling the need for exercise, and sun, Salome walked over to Billie Ruth's bakery, where she bought a chai tea and a loaf of freshly baked sour dough bread to go, then headed home.

As she approached her house, she noticed the metal flag up on the mailbox beside the street. The mail normally arrived in late afternoon. She glanced at the neighbors' boxes. No other flags were up. Puzzled, she opened the door and peered inside. She pulled out a plain cardboard box, about four inches wide and six inches long. There was nothing to indicate the sender, no postmark, not even her name. The box had some heft to it and had not been sealed.

She set the bag from Billie Ruth's on the ground and opened the box right there on the street.

A beam of sunlight hit what was nestled in tissue paper, momentarily blinding her. She closed her eyes until the bright spots faded, then, shielding the contents with the lid, looked again. She gasped. Her heart began an unhealthy staccato beat. Feeling lightheaded, she immediately plopped down on the grass.

She took the napkin from the bakery bag and carefully removed the item from the box. It was a paperweight. Etched in the glass was a quotation attributed to Albert Einstein: *Imagination is greater than knowledge.*

This was not a gift from someone wanting to remain anonymous. The paperweight loudly declared the sender— Duncan Mah. She'd last seen him in D.C., the night she'd hurled a paperweight at the back of his head. The action had been impulsive, the missile one of a collection of paperweights on a nearby table. Whether this was the actual one she'd thrown, she didn't know, since she hadn't bothered to examine it that particular night.

She placed the paperweight back in its nest of tissue and put the lid back on the box. Salome tried to quell her fear by taking a few deep breaths. The street was quiet and still. For several moments she allowed sudden anger to burn off the initial fear, then let the anger consume itself.

The Einstein quote revealed his malicious intent—that her imagination play havoc with peace of mind. Was he close by? Was he following her? Or had he passed along the paperweight to a minion—or told them to buy it— with instructions for delivery?

She sat beside the mailbox, until she finally became aware of the cold from the ground numbing her backside. She stood and stretched, then lifted her arms and flicked her two middle fingers against her thumbs to rid herself of the negative energy. He'd chosen fear as a weapon to keep her off balance, no doubt figuring that as a single woman living alone she was easy prey. The paperweight proved he was watching or having her watched and supported her own previous sense of unease. She accepted that fear would exist until he was caught and put away, but she didn't have to be consumed by it.

She collected her things, and, instead of going into the house, she hurried to the detached garage and drove to the post office. The postal clerk provided the proper envelope for an overnight delivery. Salome addressed the package to Judah Freeman's office in the District. His connections in the Metropolitan Police Department could test the paperweight and tissue for trace evidence and, hopefully, lift some prints.

Back in her truck, she used her cell phone to call Judah's office. His answering machine picked up, and she left a brief message with the numbers of her home phone and cell. Then she tried his cell phone, listening to the hollow ring until she shut off the connection.

Having brought her bakery purchases, she sipped the now cold tea, deciding to wait a few minutes should he return her call. She thought about Mah and his intentions, then tried to think *like* him. She began to feel that he probably just wanted to torment her. Killing her would only turn up the heat, increasing the effort to find him. As it was, he was currently wanted by authorities in Washington, D.C., and San Francisco in connection with homicides in those cities, and in the former, several robberies. No, she didn't think he'd try to kill her, unless she had something he wanted badly enough. Of course, that did not mean she could relax.

Just as she switched on the ignition, the cell phone rang.

"Hey, kiddo. Wazzup?" Judah's baritone was profoundly welcome.

Salome told him the news, pleased that her own voice carried no quiver of anxiety. "You should have the paperweight around noon tomorrow."

"Unless I'm in California."

"Honest, Jude, I can handle this. And you need to get the paperweight to a lab. ASAP."

"Look, hon, we're not talking one guy here. He's got plenty of folk to do his dirty work. No offense, but I think a big ole mean-lookin' black guy like me on his tail is a whole lot scarier than one of those Bagua mirrors."

Salome had a sudden, unpleasant thought. "Let me call you back. Give me five minutes." Before he could even answer, she severed the connection and sped home. Not bothering to put the truck in the garage, Salome pulled up alongside the front door and jumped out. Her eyes shot up to the space above the round, red front door.

The fear she'd managed to quell returned as raw and jagged as ever.

The Bagua mirror was gone.

Chapter 19

THE mirror had been a presence for so long she'd taken it for granted, hadn't even noticed whether or not it still hung above the door when she and Marcella had entered the house several hours earlier.

Salome went into the house, to her study, found a replacement octagonal Bagua mirror, and secured it above the front door. She took a moment to clear her mind then began the ritual. Rather than the usual nine, she increased the number of chants and stated intention—that the house and all in it were protected from harm—to twenty-seven. Once she finished, she returned Judah's call.

"While I was waiting for you to call back, I went ahead and booked a flight," he said. "I'll be arriving in San Jose around nine-fifteen."

There was no sense protesting. Once he made up his mind, it would take more effort than she was willing to expend to try and change it.

"I'll get a room near the airport and head over to your place in the morning."

"I've got a better idea. I'll pick you up, we'll grab a bite, and you can stay here at my house."

"I'm going to need a car, Salome. Most likely I'll be

doing most of the work in and around San Francisco."

"We'll get you a rental in Santa Cruz."

He gave her the name of the airline and concluded the conversation by saying, "Right. See you at nine-fifteen."

Salome went back into the house and performed the same ritual in the helpful people guas of each room. She then prepped the room adjacent to her office/study to accommodate Jude.

"I LOVE THAT LITTLE HOUSE! THERE'S EVEN A watercolor of a monarch butterfly beside my bed!"

"One of my mom's," Salome said groggily, having risen slowly to the summons at the front door the next morning.

"Mind if I check out your computer?"

"You're more than welcome to it."

They entered Salome's study, Salome shuffling behind the more energetic young woman. She and Jude had stayed up talking until after 1 A.M.

Marcella studied the components for a moment then turned on the machine. After a few minutes she exclaimed, "This is so out of date!"

"You know computers?" Salome asked, still half asleep.

"Duh! Who was my boyfriend? You need a faster processor—among other things."

Suddenly Marcella screamed. Judah filled the doorway of the adjacent study, his physical presence proof of yesterday's statement that he was scarier than a Bagua mirror.

"Marcella, this is Judah Freeman. Judah, Marcella Cruz."

Marcella swallowed hard and finally finding her voice managed a whispery "Hello."

"Sorry to startle you, Marcella."

Salome cut in. "Judah's an old friend, a private investigator in Washington, D.C. He's working on a case that required a trip to the Bay Area," Salome said, while looking at Jude, her intention clear: no further explanation necessary.

"Soon as you're ready, Mei, would you give me a lift to the nearest car rental agency?"

"Half an hour?"

"Sounds good to me."

Before leaving D.C., Jude had arranged for a homicide detective he'd mentored to pick up the paperweight at his office and take it to the lab to begin processing. They both hoped that Mah, in his effort to frighten Salome, had slipped up somehow; maybe he or an associate had left something that might be a clue to his whereabouts—possibly even the paperweight itself, such as where it was purchased. At the same time, they both accepted the fact that the man was smart enough to be as elusive as a single raindrop in a downpour.

Salome excused herself for a moment. She put on a pot of coffee, then went into her dressing room and retrieved her hairbrush. Back in the study, she began vigorously brushing her hair, a feng shui trick to raise the body ch'i and stimulate the brain.

"What did Toby think about the reopening of the institute?" she asked Marcella.

"He thought Ivy had a solid idea. But he wasn't all that interested in any of the workshops except the feng shui. He knew Ivy wanted to attract an older crowd. He wanted to give a computer workshop for people interested in learning the basics, but she vetoed that—not esoteric enough."

"Computers being his area of expertise, maybe she was pushing him away, maybe even hoping he'd leave."

"That sounds about right." Marcella looked away for a moment. "Yeah, the more I think about it—she wanted to take over. Ross probably influenced her. With Toby out of the way, they could have the property to themselves and run things as they wanted to."

"Did he make any changes to his rooms recently? You know, moving furniture around, that sort of thing?"

Marcella shook her head. "I can't think of anything in particular."

Salome had a sudden thought. "Was Toby especially fond of penguins?"

Marcella raised her eyebrows. "Penguins? Not that I know of."

"I was just thinking about the shower curtain in his bathroom."

Marcella sat a little straighter. "What shower curtain?"

"The one I saw when I went through his rooms. It looked new. Covered with penguins with the name of a company on the belly."

"Toby had a Toys for Techies shower curtain; had a bunch made up and gave them away. Promotional stuff."

"And other companies did the same thing?"

"A few of them. Toby had a couple in the closet in his bedroom. You wouldn't believe all the weird stuff that's given away."

"Well, someone hung a new one in the bath. When was the last time you were in his rooms?"

Marcella took a breath then exhaled noisily. "Probably a couple nights before he died. When Ross started coming around, Toby thought it best if we limited our meetings at night. He was sensitive about that. I think he didn't want Ivy or Ross to get the wrong impression of me. You know, that I was a slut or something."

Marcella then rose and went to the small altar set up near Salome's chair in the study's helpful people gua, featuring a small fountain and a graceful porcelain Kwan Yin statuette.

"Look, I need to shower and get dressed. Make yourself at home. I was thinking we'd go shopping. If you want to pick up anything from the institute, we can do that, too."

Biting her lip, Marcella looked away, then back at Salome.

"Can we go to the Santa Cruz library?"

"Sure. No problem. Do you have your library card?"
"It's at the house. But I won't need it."

THE THREE OF THEM PILED INTO THE TRUCK,
Jude stretching out his legs in the narrow compartment
behind the passenger seat, his briefcase and hanging bag
on his lap. Marcella scooted her seat as far forward as it
would go, to give him room, her breasts nearly touching
the glove compartment.

Salome first drove to a car rental agency in Santa Cruz,
and she and Marcella waited while Judah picked up a car.
Before heading off to San Francisco, he and Salome stood
outside her truck talking for a few moments. Last night
he'd booked a room in a small hotel not far from City
Lights bookstore and made arrangements to meet an old
friend, also retired and formerly with the San Francisco
Police Department. Salome had offered him the use of a
town house her parents owned on Nob Hill, which was
used by family members whenever they wanted to take
advantage of the city's many amenities. Judah declined
the offer. And though he did not say so, she figured he
didn't want to be responsible for property damage, should
he attract and encounter any bad guys.

"If you need money, Jude, just ask. San Francisco can
surely eat up the bucks," Salome said, as he started to
amble toward his rental. "And you're always welcome at
my place."

"We know Mah has connections in San Francisco. So
that's the place to look first. As far as money goes, I'm
cool. Only thing bothers me is that I didn't take care of
this business sooner."

Salome moved back behind the wheel of her truck. Judah raised his hand and waved. "I'll be in touch."

"That guy's something else," Marcella observed, after
Salome pulled out into traffic. "Not someone you'd want
as an enemy."

"He's one of those people who will put himself in harm's way for a friend."

"Is that why he's here? Putting himself in harm's way for you?"

Salome didn't answer immediately. "Let's just say he's looking into something for me," she finally said, then changed the subject. "So, what's at the library?"

Like Salome, Marcella was not forthcoming with details.

ABOUT TWENTY MINUTES LATER, SALOME parked in the public lot just off Pacific Avenue, her curiosity piqued. But Marcella had remained silent during the drive, saying nothing about her reason for wanting to go to the library, which apparently didn't include checking out any books.

A moment after they entered, passing by the checkout positions to the right, Marcella turned left and into the room devoted to California history and genealogy.

She stopped at a free-standing wooden bookcase about four feet tall in the center of the room.

"Pick out a book," Marcella said, pointing to several reference volumes on the top shelf and immediately stooping down. Salome complied and began casually leafing through a large-format book. The librarian stood at her desk up ahead and to the right, talking to another patron. Salome feigned interest in the pages, keeping one eye on Marcella, who was on her knees, reaching beneath the bottom shelf.

Salome jumped when she heard a ripping sound and coughed to cover the noise. The librarian glanced over at her. Salome coughed again, and the librarian resumed her quiet conversation.

"Let's go!" Marcella whispered, slipping something into her pocket.

Salome closed the book and returned it to the shelf.

They walked over to one of the coffeehouses on Pacific

Avenue, Marcella not speaking until they were seated in the back, each with a fresh breakfast muffin and a cup of specialty coffee, a buffer of empty tables between them and the other patrons. Most people were occupying the outside tables anyway, enjoying the sun shining on the passing parade.

Marcella withdrew a plastic-wrapped cardboard mailer about three inches by five. She peeled off the duct tape that had been used to secure it to the bottom of the bookshelf and wrapped it in a ball for disposal. Opening the mailer, she removed what looked like a shiny business card with rounded sides protected by a clear plastic sleeve. It was smaller than the mailer.

"This is the disc Toby gave me to hide in the library— one of the things I did that day I spent in Santa Cruz. God, the last time I saw him alive, he gave me this," she moaned, slipping the disc back into the mailer.

"What's on it?"

"I don't know. But its got to be important. He told me it would be insurance if anything happened to him. And then, I was only to show it to someone I trusted."

Marcella continued after wiping a tear from her cheek. "He said if the police were involved not to simply hand it over but to look around for a good lawyer—and even then use caution.

"He didn't leave me many options. But, hell, I didn't take it seriously, never believing I'd ever be in this position." She rubbed the mailer, her eyes mournful.

"Well," Salome said excitedly, "let's head back to my house and take a look."

"I doubt if you have the right software."

"Then we'll get the right software. We can drive on over to Fry's."

"It's not that easy, Salome. And I don't think using your machine is such a good idea, anyway."

"Why not?"

"Because. When you're on the computer, you never know who's watching."

Salome found the statement chilling. For all their convenience, computers had the capacity to be quite frightening.

Back at the house, Marcella sat in front of the computer, just staring at the monitor and the Bagua Salome used as the screen's wallpaper. The disc remained in the mailer to the right of the keyboard.

"Toby told me the disc has web links," Marcella finally said, "which means we have to connect to the web. What scares me is that it might send a warning signal to a different computer and then we could be tracked down."

"Surely Toby would have protected it some way."

"Yeah. But the thing is, I just don't know. If he hacked into someone's files, and those files have embedded warning systems, then no telling what could happen. Hell, the FBI might show up."

"Then what are we going to do? You think Monk or Wizard or Gnome might help?"

"They're wimps. Didn't they split, leaving Toby alone with the consequences?"

"You have any other ideas?"

Suddenly, a smile grew on Marcella's face, and her eyes actually twinkled with mischief. Salome couldn't imagine what had prompted this radical change in her demeanor.

"I do. But I don't think you're going to like it."

Chapter 20

MARCELLA was right. Salome did not like the proposition but had to agree when Marcella said Toby would probably sit up in his grave and applaud—at least in theory. Of course, Toby no longer had worries.

"Marcella, he wanted to protect you—not send you into the lion's den."

"Look, the system is probably still connected in his home office. The police confiscated his hard drive and such, but if we can get a laptop with the same software he had, all we have to do is set up."

"*Break in* and set up, Marcella."

"Don't you see, if it can be traced, it'll be traced right to his office—like he's communicating from the grave."

She sat forward and smiled. "Hey, I understand your reluctance. And I don't want to get you in trouble. I'll just do it myself."

Salome ignored the last statement. "Tomorrow night, my cousin and Detective Child are having a party at the Fairmont in San Jose. Most likely Ross and Ivy will attend."

Salome left her chair and moved to the side of the desk. She picked up the telephone and punched out Phyllis's number at the Holyrood police station. She reached the secretary first, then Phyllis came on the line.

"I was thinking of calling you—but that meant that I'd actually have to speak to you," Phyllis said angrily.

"I'm just checking on the time of your party tomorrow night."

"You might rethink coming. Gordon won't be happy to see you. Neither will Ivy Ashcroft or Ross Prenderville. I cannot believe you actually bailed out Marcella Cruz!"

That was all she needed to know.

"Are you mad at me, too?"

"What do you think?"

"Maybe I should reconsider the wedding gift I'd planned to give you."

"And what would that be?"

"The Perfume Mansion."

Dead silence filled the line.

"Talk to you later, Phyl." Salome hung up.

That would give her cousin something to think about.

"Ross and Ivy will be at the Fairmont tomorrow night. Now, let's take care of shopping chores."

Salome had plenty of black clothing, so it was a matter of outfitting Marcella and buying toiletries and items she'd need for the next few days—and definitely a new coat. Hopefully, whatever was on the mysterious disc would be enough to eliminate Marcella as a suspect—and point the finger at the real killer.

Fry's Electronics had the best deals and selections, so Salome drove back over the Santa Cruz Mountains, allowing Marcella to choose the equipment, a lightweight laptop with all the bells and whistles. Salome needed a new one anyway, having not yet replaced the one that had been stolen during a chaotic round of speaking engagements earlier in the year.

After dinner that night and after Marcella was tucked away in the tiny cottage at Otter Haven, Salome stared at the luminous image of Kwan Yin, while stretched out on the futon.

She considered calling Marybeth—for all of two seconds. Since she and Marcella planned to circumvent the law, to put it mildly, Marybeth would not be a sympathetic listener. However, if anything went wrong, Salome, too, would need a lawyer. *Cross that bridge when I come to it,* Salome thought.

Unless Ivy had gone to the trouble of installing a security system, Marcella seemed to think they'd encounter no problems entering the house. Toby's bathroom window, she'd said, was always open a crack. Given Ivy's dislike of spending money, the chances of encountering a new alarm were few—according to Marcella. Salome hoped Marcella was right.

They set out at 6:30 the following evening. That afternoon, Salome had taken the pickup to a trusted mechanic to make certain it was in tip-top condition, not wanting any surprises in that arena.

The traffic was typically heavy for a Friday night then petered out when they entered the coastal highway. Neither of them said much. Marcella sat with a black canvas bag on her lap containing the computer and the disc and their cotton gloves. Marcella's fingerprints had already been found in the house, and even Salome had touched various things in Toby's rooms the day Ivy raced her through the feng shui consultation. But it would be best not to leave fresh prints.

Passing the long drive up to the Big House, the sign for the Star Institute now retired, Salome did as Marcella directed and turned right onto another road on the north side of the pumpkin patch. The dirt road led up through the pine trees and over the hill into a pasture. Again, at Marcella's instruction, Salome parked off to the side in a copse.

After she pocketed the car key and moved around the truck to join Marcella, her companion said softly, "Watch out for cow patties." And with that, they set out.

In their black clothing, they melted into the shadows, and in a matter of minutes stood on the northeast side of the Playhouse. Across open ground was the Big House, dark but for the porch light.

"Just follow me," Marcella whispered.

Maybe because of her Indian blood, Marcella seemed to instinctively know how to move without making a sound as she hunched down and crept toward the rose-bushes in front of Toby's rooms. They'd have to be careful not to snag their clothes on the thorns. Salome followed, mimicking Marcella's stealthy movements, until they stopped just below the bathroom window between Toby's bedroom and office. Marcella took the cotton gloves out of the bag. They each pulled on a pair.

The bathroom window was about six feet off the ground, no surprise, as Marcella had mentioned it earlier when going over exactly what they would do when they arrived at the house. Salome bent over, and Marcella stepped up onto her back. The moment of truth had arrived. Salome steeled herself for the blare of an alarm. With the exception of the scrape of the window being pushed upward, no other sound shattered the quiet.

In seconds, Salome was relieved of Marcella's weight. A moment later, Marcella unlatched the nearest bedroom window.

"Careful of the rosebushes," Marcella whispered, then helped Salome inside, closing and latching the window afterward.

They passed Toby's bed—Marcella touched a pillow, maybe for luck. Salome followed Marcella through the bathroom and into the blackness of Toby's office. Marcella switched on the penlight and began examining the wainscoting behind the desk. A moment later, she rose and, still without a word, set up the laptop. Using the length of cord attached to the portable computer, she plugged it into the telephone jack.

"Fingers crossed," she said softly and went to work. A couple seconds later, the screen came on, bathing Marcella's face in blue light. Marcella pumped her fist and grinned. Then she sent Salome back into the bedroom to stand lookout.

The wait seemed interminable. After awhile, Salome heard Marcella cry out and dashed into the office. Marcella shooed her away. Salome glanced at the screen and saw what looked like computer animation. Her heart sank. What if this was just a computer game Toby had designed. Still, he wouldn't have gone to so much trouble to hide it.

Maybe fifteen minutes had gone by when she suddenly noticed headlights on the drive approaching the house. She hurried back to the office.

"Someone's coming."

Marcella looked up momentarily. "See who it is."

"Marcella! Turn off the damn machine."

"I just need a couple minutes."

"We don't *have* a couple minutes!"

Salome ran back into the bedroom. Standing to the side of the window, she glanced outside. A sedan with the logo of a security firm on the passenger door stopped between the Playhouse and the Big House. A man wearing a dark uniform got out of the car and switched on a flashlight. He was alone.

Salome returned to the office. "Now!" she hissed.

Marcella unplugged the laptop, and seeming to take forever, repacked the equipment. Salome went back into the bedroom and ducked just as a light shown in the window. A moment later, she felt Marcella on the floor beside her.

The light moved off.

Salome pressed her mouth to Marcella's ear. "Did you close the bathroom window?"

Marcella nodded.

They heard movement around the side of the house, and then the security guard returned and passed by the windows. Marcella rose and at a crouch moved over to the west window.

Salome now questioned her sanity—here I am with a suspect in a murder investigation, breaking and entering the house of the victim. Good-bye reputation, hello jail time!

Marcella came back and helped Salome to her feet.

"He's headed down to the institute."

"Maybe we tripped a silent alarm," Salome whispered and moved into the bathroom.

"He's probably just checking the place out. Ivy and Ross maybe figured I'd come back and arranged for a security guy to stop by when they're out."

"I wish you'd mentioned that before."

In the bathroom, Marcella crawled out the window first. Salome handed down the canvas bag, then Marcella helped Salome to the ground. They then repeated the original routine, whereby Marcella climbed onto Salome's back and closed the window, leaving a small space open at the top. With each passing moment, Salome was sure they'd be caught. Avoiding open ground between the Playhouse and the Big House, Marcella lead Salome along the side of the house and down the hill. Their luck held, and, hunched down, they cut across open pasture and back to the truck, where they waited inside the cab until they saw the headlights of the security car shoot out to the east. Once the headlights disappeared, Salome started the engine.

Rather than turn back to the highway and risk passing the security car on the dirt road, Marcella told Salome to drive on past the dairy. Finally they came to a paved road and turned north. And so, using a roundabout route, they returned to Highway 1, heading south.

"I made a copy," Marcella said, after explaining excitedly that the disc contained Ross Prenderville's files, which Toby had incorporated into a game. "He calls it 'The Greatest Treasure,' and it's like an adult version of *Where in the World Is Carmen Sandiego?*"

"The greatest treasure—hey, that's from 'October Song,'" Salome noted, having read the lyrics so many times they were practically committed to memory. "Rather ironic, since that's what Prenderville sang at the presentation dinner."

"He must have been embezzling from the get-go, hiding money in accounts all over the place. Toby being Toby embedded those files in a game."

Marcella shook her head. "Looks like Ross used Toys for Techies as training ground to become a cyber criminal. Now we've got to get this disc to the right people."

"Why didn't Toby simply take the information to the proper authorities in the first place?"

Marcella jerked her head around. "You don't understand, do you?" Her voice was strident, her tone defensive. Anger, too, fired the outburst but was not, Salome thought, directed at her but at Toby.

"Money was just part of the game. Having money all his life made it meaningless. Only the game counted. And that bastard Prenderville—the stealing—Toby just saw it as fun; the foundation for a new game."

"Yes, but also as a trap, Marcella."

Marcella sighed, her anger spent.

Salome quickly redirected the conversation.

"How about taking the disc to Detective Childs?"

"No way."

"You're sure?"

"That's just it. I'm not sure. About anyone."

When they crossed into the city of Santa Cruz, Salome pulled over into the parking lot of a fast-food restaurant. Retrieving her cell phone and Dicken's business card, she asked, "What about Dicken Fowler?"

"God. I don't know." Marcella took a deep breath. "Yeah. Okay."

Salome called the number, remembering to use the name Mijo Koyama. "I've got something for you that will void those lawsuits and put the blame for the demise of Toys for Techies right where it belongs."

NEARLY AN HOUR LATER, SALOME PULLED into the parking lot of the same family restaurant on Hamilton Avenue, where she had first met the three techies.

While looking for a parking space, she noticed a gold Lexus, with someone seated behind the wheel facing the street. Familiar enough with the car now, she knew who that someone happened to be.

"Get down!" she cried. Prenderville knew what kind of car she drove, but would be expecting Mijo Koyama to meet Dicken. Dicken must have called him. The only reason she could think of was to sell the disc, maybe use it as blackmail. When she'd talked to him in the restaurant with his buddies, his dislike for Prenderville seemed quite genuine. In any case, the presence of Ross Prenderville changed the plan. She drove around the restaurant then reentered traffic on Hamilton Avenue.

There was still one person she could trust to be on the side of truth and justice, one person she could trust with the disc.

THE ENGAGEMENT PARTY WAS BEING HELD IN one of the meeting rooms at the posh Fairmont Hotel. But Salome didn't intend to join the partygoers. Using hotel stationery, she wrote a note, wrapped it around the packet containing the disc, slipped it into an envelope, wrote Phyllis's name on the outside, then gave it to the concierge with a twenty-dollar bill and asked him to deliver it personally. She waited until he returned, mission accomplished, then went back to the car and drove home.

"The Greatest Treasure" was a good title for Toby's game, but, considering the information it held, "Pandora's Box" would have been appropriate, too.

Chapter 21

SINCE Marcella had tenanted the Playhouse for the past two years, Detective Child wanted her present when he fulfilled the specifics of the search warrant on the Monday after his and Phyllis's engagement party. Salome drove Marcella to the estate, where various vehicles, including a police cruiser, were parked between the Big House and the Playhouse. Ross Prenderville's Lexus was not there. Both Salome and Marcella tried to hide the nervousness they'd experienced all weekend while waiting for something to happen.

Child and two uniformed cops stood in the living room. Ivy sat stiffly on the futon couch, that poison arrow from the fireplace directed right at her.

Child instructed Ivy to open the safe.

Ivy went to the fireplace and pressed the button behind a family picture that was hanging on the adjoining wall.

"You found the murder weapon. What more do you want?" Ivy intoned, her expression sour.

Not bothering to answer, Detective Child simply gave her a bland look that belied the message in his alert stance, the tension in his torso and legs that of a hunter watching prey approach a trap.

After the loud clicking sound, Ivy pulled back a portion of the brick wedge.

Child moved beside Ivy and, with a flashlight, peered into the darkness. From where Salome stood beside the couch, she could see that it was a little more than a foot deep—and empty.

"You can see there's nothing in there," Ivy said. "You've got the murder weapon. This is a waste of time."

"Oh there's something else in here, all right," Child said. A moment later, they all heard another click, like a spring releasing. Then he pulled out a small camera.

Child said to the room in general, "I'll be right back."

Detective Child left, and his departure seemed to suck all the air out of the room. Ivy stared straight ahead. Marcella appeared baffled. Salome tried to contain her excitement, while the two uniforms looked bored as statues.

A few minutes later, Detective Child strode back into the room. He looked pointedly at Marcella. Salome groaned inwardly, fearing for her friend. But the detective stopped in front of Ivy.

"Ms. Ashcroft, would you please show me your hands?"

Reluctantly, Ivy held out her hands, the diamond sparkling on the third finger of her left hand. Taking a deep breath, Detective Child then turned to Marcella and asked the same of her.

With a satisfied expression, he then began to read Ivy Ashcroft her rights and arrested her for the murder of her brother.

Ivy opened her mouth to speak but abruptly shut it, maybe thinking it would be best to "remain silent."

When the uniforms escorted Ivy to the squad car, Detective Child spoke to Marcella. "You're lucky you're not into diamonds." He explained that a small infrared camera had been installed behind a tiny peephole at the back of the safe. Putting it simply, he said the button that opened the safe was attached to a wire that silently activated the camera. The images were stored digitally, and thousands could be collected. When the safe was shut, the camera stopped taking pictures.

Before the images of Child reaching in to remove the camera were those of Ivy as she had opened the safe, then shots of him pulling out the murder weapon wrapped in the bloody rag. And just before that, the camera recorded hands covered in latex gloves removing some papers and placing the blood-stained bundle inside. Though only the torso could be seen, Ivy's distinctive diamond was unmistakable, stretching the latex on her ring finger.

"We'll need to talk to you again, so don't go too far. I understand you're staying with Salome."

"That's right."

"It'll be a few days before you can come back. Apparently there was a new will among those papers taken out of the safe."

"How do you know that?"

He regarded her in silence for a moment, then said, "I'll just say this: we found a certain computer disc of Toby's. Among other things on the disc was a file containing a will and the location of the will in the safe. The day I opened the safe and found the murder weapon there were no papers inside, as you no doubt remember. Someone had obviously removed them, someone who knew about the location of the safe—Ivy. Then I got to thinking about the safe itself, that it might have extra features as some do nowadays. Toby Ashcroft, being a man who liked gadgets, I figured he'd probably rigged up something. I was right."

"So who actually killed Toby?" Marcella blurted.

Again, he gave her a contemplative look but no answer this time. "You're free to go, Marcella."

Marcella and Salome started for the door.

"Oh, and no hard feelings I hope," Detective Child said.

When they were outside, Salome said, "Did you know about the safe?"

Marcella shrugged. "When we were kids it was just a secret place where Toby and Ivy put stuff. After I moved back, I didn't even think about it, and Toby never used it when I was around."

"The will must be in your favor, Marcella," Salome said once they were back on the road.

"Why do you say that?"

"I could say because it was in the family gua and you were certainly family to Toby. But more than anything it was Detective Child's last remark."

"No hard feelings?"

"You are a voter, Marcella, and even, I daresay, a potential campaign contributor."

When they returned to Salome's, there was a message from Jude. He'd called only once since he'd been in San Francisco, and then just to give her the phone number of his friend, Herschel Harris, the retired cop. Herschel was a widower and owned a condo in the Marina District. He insisted that Jude stay in his spare bedroom. Jude had no qualms about staying with a fellow cop.

Salome introduced herself to the man who answered the phone, presumably Harris. "Is Jude around?"

A moment later, Jude picked up. "Made some progress, kiddo. The Chinese art and antiquities shops owned by the real Duncan Mah did very well until around the time the British gave Hong Kong back to the Chinese, when people began leaving in droves. The market was flooded with products and prices plummeted. Mah just managed to hang on. Then last year he decided to sell the business.

"I talked to a Chinatown cop this afternoon. He's pretty certain that's when the impostor appeared, got friendly, made an offer on all the shops—let's see, in Montreal, New York, and here in San Francisco—never intending to buy. He did want the shops, though, as they would provide a perfect front to move people—the illegals he was charging a fortune to smuggle into the U.S. and Canada—and drugs.

"And the real Mah was one of the few people in Chinatown who didn't have a big family around. Originally from Hong Kong, both parents deceased, never married.

His only living relative, your neighbor in Georgetown . . . that is, until she died last year. Anyway, the impostor saw an opportunity, murdered Mah, and took over his identity. He fired the staff at each store and put his people in—all done over the phone. By the way, the shop in Georgetown he put his own money into but used stock from the other stores.

"Scuttlebutt in Chinatown is that he's a guy by the name of James Wong, a former member of one of the Hong Kong gangs—tongs, I guess you call them. Father British, mother Chinese. And, like you speculated a while back, they figure he's setting up his own little criminal empire."

"Has anyone seen him recently?"

"As a matter of fact, yes. And here we have the good news. A local snitch said he'd been in San Francisco last week. But, for some reason, he left suddenly for Montreal. No doubt traveling under another alias. So he's gone."

"Do the cops believe the snitch?"

"As far as snitches go, they say his information is pretty reliable. The fact that he didn't come forward until *after* Mah/Wong, left town makes me think he's telling the truth."

Salome felt some relief, though not enough to allow her to completely relax. "Good work, Jude. And what are your plans?"

"Think I'll hang around for a few more days. Follow up on a couple leads. Hit a few jazz clubs, maybe take in a play. Plus it's great to spend some time with my old buddy."

"Well, keep me posted."

"You got it. Oh—almost forgot. The bad news. The lab didn't find anything of interest on that paperweight. Not even a fingerprint."

"Phooey!"

"Hey. It was worth a try. Don't you worry. We'll nail the guy."

* * *

THAT EVENING REGGIE TELEPHONED, HIS voice anxious.

"Salome, you cannot give the Perfume to Phyllis as a wedding present."

"Dad, please don't—"

Before she could finish, he jumped back in. "It just occurred to me. It's all well and good that the man she's marrying has political aspirations, but hell! He'll sell the place to finance his campaign!"

"Phyllis wouldn't allow it."

"She's in love, Salome, and in that state she cannot be trusted!"

OVER THE NEXT FEW DAYS, THE DETAILS OF the Ashcroft murder came to light.

After closing the pumpkin stand and piling the scarecrows in the back of the pickup, Toby Ashcroft would drive to the Big House, drop his keys, the money box, and carving knife on the table in the foyer, take off his shoes, wash his hands and face, strip down to long underwear, and head for his computer. He would read and answer E-mail then lose himself in a computer game. (At the time of his death, he'd been playing Civilization II, a role-playing game of world domination.) Sometime around 11 P.M., he would shower and go to bed.

This much Marcella, Ivy Ashcroft, and Ross Prenderville agreed on, the computer activity was confirmed by authorities working on his hard drive, particularly the times he logged on and off.

The last time he logged off was at 10:58 P.M. on the night of October 29.

Shortly afterward, when Toby began to shower, Ross Prenderville approached him from behind and slit his throat with the carving knife he'd taken from the table in the foyer. Besides the knife, Prenderville brought a bucket with a lid, which he used to collect blood from the gushing wound. Some of the blood he used to stain the scarecrow mask. Leaving the body in the bathtub, Prenderville walked down to the pumpkin patch and poured out the blood behind a bale of hay before it congealed.

At 5 A.M., he dressed the body in the scarecrow outfit and carried it to Toby's pickup, where he added the corpse to the scarecrows under a tarp in the truck bed. He drove to the pumpkin patch and positioned Toby with his head over the blood-stained ground, put up the scarecrows, set out the jack-o'-lanterns, and arranged the stand to appear that Toby had been working before he was killed.

Ivy, meanwhile, slipped on a pair of latex gloves from a box Toby kept handy for use when he worked on the bowels of his computers, cleaned the murder scene, hung a new shower curtain, and wrapped the carving knife in a blood-soaked rag. Knowing that Marcella had spent the night in Santa Cruz, she carried the rag and murder weapon in a plastic grocery bag to the Playhouse, took it out of the bag, and made the deposit in the safe, at the same time removing the papers.

Finally, Ivy drove Prenderville back to Davenport and let him off a couple of blocks from his house, which he entered as he'd left the previous night, through the back door. She tossed the money box that Toby kept at the stand, the bucket, shower curtain, and various sponges and towels and latex gloves in a restaurant Dumpster and drove home to prepare for a day in San Francisco.

Prenderville confessed quickly, trying to make a deal. Ivy spoke to no one but her lawyer. When the information on the disc was revealed, Ivy Ashcroft seemed genuinely stunned, apparently unaware of the extent of her fiancé's greed, and finally opened up, saying it was Prenderville's idea to "get Toby out of the way," so she could collect the millions from the sale of the estate, but not for the dairy.

* * *

JUDE'S SLEUTHING YIELDED LITTLE MORE about the man Salome would always think of as Duncan Mah. The Chinatown cop had shared all he knew, and the locals would not talk to a non-Chinese stranger. The Chinese community was quite insular, and even if Jude had been fluent in Mandarin or Cantonese, it was doubtful anyone would have opened up to him. On the Wednesday following Ivy's arrest, Jude drove back to Santa Cruz to return the rental. Salome took him to the airport to catch his flight to Washington. The short trip to the west coast seemed to have done him good. He was in high spirits and spoke with confidence about tracking down Mah/Wong. She sensed that he had learned something more, maybe something too sketchy to share at the moment.

DETECTIVE CHILD COULDN'T HAVE ASKED for better publicity and certainly had plenty to be thankful for over the Thanksgiving holiday. The bizarre nature of the crime—the fratricide, the Halloween theme, the vast amounts of money involved, the computer-related issues, the New Age involvement—all served to attract national attention. While his name was still fresh in the minds of Californians, he announced his plans to run for governor. Though some accused him of taking advantage of a man's brutal murder to launch his career, the realists agreed that, if nothing else, a politician is an opportunist.

PHYLLIS CAME OVER ONE EVENING AFTER Marcella had returned to the Ashcroft estate. Over a couple of beers she and Salome chatted—amicably, for a change.

"Prenderville has implicated some techie." She paused, apparently searching for a name that, had Salome been so inclined, she could have supplied. "Ah. Fowler, Dicken Fowler. Said he provided the know-how to hide money."

"What does Fowler say?"

"What else? He denies it."

"And Gordon? What does he think?"

"That Prenderville's grasping. Hell, he's not a novice; got his undergraduate degree in computer science. And his house is full of state-of-the-art computer equipment, most likely pilfered from the institute."

Gradually, the conversation turned from murder to the gentler subject of love. Phyllis, of course, was full of it—love, that is—and wanted the world, specifically Salome, to also feast at the table.

"When are you going to get something going with Michael O'Kelly? I know you love each other."

Taken by surprise, Salome didn't know how to respond. Then, after a moment's consideration she said, "Love? Maybe what I want is the sort of intimacy that comes when the emotions step aside and simple, honest feelings comfortably blend with those of another. The operative word here is *comfortably*."

"Well, you need to spend time together to reach the comfort zone, Mei."

LATER, AS THEY STOOD AT THE DOOR, PHYLlis said, "Look, I want to thank you for offering the Perfume as a wedding gift."

"You always loved the place, and it's as good a time as any for a change in owners."

Phyllis smiled. "Thing is, Salome, I'm turning it down."

Salome was stunned. Then she wondered if her father had talked to Phyllis but couldn't really ask without having to explain Reggie's reservations.

"But why?"

"Oh, I don't know. The Ashcroft case has been a damn good lesson in greed and ambition. Know what I think? I think Prenderville would have gotten rid of Ivy eventually so as to have complete control of the Ashcroft estate. And to think, he was really hot on backing Gordon for governor. Hell, Prenderville probably had his own hidden agenda there, too. No telling what sort of scandal he might have gotten Gordon involved in.

"Anyway, I'm going to be dealing with ambitious people, and I just don't want to tempt fate by moving into the Perfume. I don't think Gordon and I would really be happy there."

After Phyllis left, Salome considered what Phyllis had said and wondered if, without mentioning it, she'd remembered the feng shui of the mansion and the missing relationship gua, which underscored the history of place. Marriages just didn't work out in the Perfume. The previous year, Salome had implemented cures, but apparently Phyllis didn't want to take any chances, and her marriage meant more than a multimillion-dollar piece of property. Reggie would be happy.

EARLY THE NEXT MORNING, SALOME PUT her Drizabone over her nightclothes and went outside in the rain to the two redwoods located in the relationship gua of the property as a whole. Sitting with the ragged burnished red bark at her back, the branches extended protectively overhead, she felt right at home, and in the coat of a similar color, she blended into the landscape. Through the misty veil, she regarded the metallic-looking bay, refusing to let the menace of Duncan Mah affect her every action.

But she hadn't been there five minutes, when the tranquillity was abruptly interrupted.

"Ah, the feng shui lady. Or as Phyl would say, the house witch."

Startled, Salome looked up to see, of all people, Michael O'Kelly standing there wearing a black wet suit with a blue stripe down the arms and legs.

Quickly recovering her composure, she said lightly, "You're dressed for the weather."

"Been surfing. Came right up from the beach."

"Where's your board?"

Not waiting for an invitation, he plopped down beside her and said briskly, "I let some kid borrow it. Look, I wanted to apologize for my behavior at the Beach Bistro. I was a little abrupt."

"Did you have some sort of epiphany at sea?"

Ignoring the remark, he went on, "Salome . . . I . . ."

"What?"

He looked away. "Emily Harkin's coming back from vacation today."

Emily was the managing editor of the *Holyrood Echo*, and a nosy neighbor, who found Salome a bit too interesting.

"No wonder it's been so peaceful around here."

"Anyway, with her back at the paper, I'll be free for a while."

"Planning on going back to Boston?"

"Oh that. No."

An awkward silence descended. Apparently, he was waiting for her to say something. "How's your mother?"

"Good as can be expected. She doesn't recognize me anymore."

"Must be awful, Michael. I can't imagine."

Another silence fell, this one less edgy.

Finally, Michael said, "I've come across a house you might be interested in feng shuiing."

"Really?" She perked.

"Yeah. Even has a name. Rosehall."

She thought for a moment but could not recall a house of that name and wondered what he was getting at. "Must not be around here. Is it in Monterey?"

"Further south." Still looking out at the water, he went on. "Anyway, if you have some time, I thought you might like to take a look."

"That could be arranged but, come on, Michael, where is it?"

Michael placed his hand on hers, instantly claiming her

attention, his smile both mischievous and captivating. "Jamaica."

"Jamaica?"

Just days ago, she'd gone through the house stimulating the helpful people guas. Had she forgotten? The helpful people gua also included *travel*. She nearly laughed.

My, my, she thought. If she really wanted to get comfortable with this man, maybe Jamacia was the place to do it, far from the traps of their personal history. And, as she had done so many times, Salome marveled at the mysterious ways of ch'i.

Epilogue

☯

MONTHS later, John Gray settled into his favorite chair with a cup of coffee and opened the newspaper.

"Well, I'll be damned!" he exclaimed, attracting his daughter Gigi's attention. He read the story about the final settlement of the Ashcroft estate and the new owner.

Gigi climbed up over the arm of the chair and stared at the picture of a beaming Marcella Cruz holding a baby. Gigi reached out and pointed to the freshly painted residence looming behind Marcella.

"Look Daddy, Big House!"